Ninja Timmy

WRITTEN AND ILLUSTRATED BY
HENRIK TAMM

DELACORTE PRESS

All rights reserved. Published in the United States by Delacorte Press, an imprint of Random House Children's Books, a division of Penguin Random House LLC, New York. This English-language work was first published in Sweden as a Swedish translation by Bonnier Carlsen as *Ninja Timmy Och De Stulna Skratten*, copyright © 2013 by Henrik Tamm. The U.S. publication in the English language is by arrangement with Bonnierforlagen, Stockholm, Sweden.

Delacorte Press is a registered trademark and the colophon is a trademark of Penguin Random House LLC.

Visit us on the Web! randomhousekids.com

Educators and librarians, for a variety of teaching tools, visit us at RHTeachersLibrarians.com

Library of Congress Cataloging-in-Publication Data
Tamm, Henrik.
[Ninja Timmy och de stulna skratten. English]
Ninja Timmy / Henrik Tamm.
pages cm
Originally published in Swedish by Bonnier Carlsen in 2013 under title:
Ninja Timmy och de stulna skratten.
Summary: In the city of Elyzandrium, an intrepid cat and his animal friends meet an inventor of magical toys, investigate the case of the stolen laughter, and ultimately become a successful crime fighting gang of ninjas.
ISBN 978-0-385-74451-5 (trade hc) — ISBN 978-0-375-99170-7 (library binding) — ISBN 978-0-385-39021-7 (ebook) [1. Cats—Fiction. 2. Animals—Fiction. 3. Friendship—Fiction. 4. Magic—Fiction. 5. Ninjas—Fiction.] I. Title.
PZ7.1.T36Ni 2015
[Fic]—dc23
2014025073

Printed in China
10 9 8 7 6 5 4 3 2 1
First American Edition

For Vilma and Hjalmar

Ninja Timmy

Chapter 1

TIMMY'S BRIGHT YELLOW eyes narrowed as he peered at the brass hinge he was trying to attach to the complex wooden framework. Again he twisted the screwdriver, slowly screwing the hinge into place. *There.* He could feel the metal grooves of the screw join with the metal grooves of the hinge and sink into the wood.

"Ah yes. Quite nice."

Pleased, he looked around for another hinge.

Timmy was a cat, not quite fully grown yet, but definitely not a kitten. He liked to think of himself as pretty clever for his age, as well as strong-minded and very inventive.

It was midafternoon. He and his pal Simon the mink were working in the loft above the bakery where they stayed and also where they invented and built things. Once, they had invented a device for spreading the perfect glaze over the baker's pastries, and as payment the baker had given them the use of the empty room upstairs.

Simon was a year older than Timmy, but they had known each other for as long as they could remember. They'd become friends in an orphanage, back when neither of them had had a real home, and they had looked out for each other ever since. Simon was a handsome mink—at least, he kept pointing that out—and spent an hour or more a day grooming himself. He had an easy time with girls, and there was always some cute mink girl or some big-eyed squirrel girl coming around the loft to visit him. Timmy didn't know how Simon did

it. He himself had always been shy with those puzzling creatures and silently wished some of Simon's confidence would rub off on him. Timmy was confident in many ways, but girls were simply a mystery to him.

It was a warm afternoon. Through the open window they could see the bustle of the city below. Elyzandrium was its name, and it was sprawled across a valley and enclosed on all sides by high, forested mountains. Fantastical three-hundred-foot bamboo towers soared into the sky, and smoke billowed from ten thousand chimneys on buildings between them. A million vehicles of all kinds clogged the dusty streets, and the sky buzzed with steam-powered balloons and other strange-looking flying machines.

Simon and Timmy were too busy to enjoy the view today, though. Their latest invention, a machine that could automatically peel oranges, was almost finished. It was a big thing, made from pieces of wood they had found around town. All its parts had been recycled. The brass fasteners, for example, had come from some old bicycles they had rescued from a scrap yard.

The machine was so big, in fact, that Timmy was wondering how they would ever get it downstairs. They were planning to sell it to one of the local fruit merchants, who wanted to start selling juice.

Timmy furrowed his brow. "You got an extra hinge over there?" he asked Simon.

Simon looked around, grabbed an extra hinge, and tossed it over to Timmy.

"Don't fasten it too tight, like last time, or the plugs will come out," Simon murmured, concentrating on the work in front of him.

Timmy smiled.

"It has to be tight, or the spring-loaded thingamajig won't engage," he replied confidently. "And, my mink friend, it's your job to make sure the wooden plugs stay in place." He paused and grinned. "Just use lots of glue."

Simon muttered to himself, but he knew Timmy was right. He filled each hole to the rim with glue and then pushed the plugs into place.

"When are Jasper and Casper gonna show up, anyway?" he asked. "We need their strength to carry this thing downstairs."

"Should be back any minute. They're just collecting sap for the varnish."

And at that very moment, the two brothers clambered up the stairs. Jasper and Casper were piglets and, quite naturally, were a little plump. And, as pigs usually were, they were really good at math. They both carried notepads around so they could quickly come up with answers to tricky questions. Unfortunately, they seldom came up with the same answer and would squabble endlessly about who was right.

Timmy and Simon had known the piglet brothers for a couple of years now, ever since meeting them at a science fair. The brothers had helped them with some of the calculations needed for one of their inventions, and they had all become fast friends. Now Jasper and Casper were an integral part of the team. Because of their weight, they were also useful in other ways.

Timmy grinned as they entered the room.

"Good. There you are. Here, come over and sit on this."

Both Jasper and Casper wandered over and plunked themselves down on a piece of the machine's frame. The wood groaned under their weight as Timmy quickly and gingerly twisted in the last screw.

"Done!" he exclaimed happily. "Our automated orange peeler is complete! Looks quite nice, doesn't it? Just the varnish left."

Timmy, Simon, and the two piglets stepped back and looked at their creation proudly.

As the sun started to set, the four friends lumbered down the stairs with their contraption. Timmy and Simon carried the front, while Jasper and Casper took the brunt of the weight at the back. They all huffed and puffed, pausing momentarily on a landing to catch their breath.

The baker's six-year-old daughter, Mathilda, watched them curiously from the back doorway of the bakery.

"Mathilda!" Timmy called. "We haven't seen you in ages. We were wondering where you've been."

"Yeah, Mathilda," Simon chimed in. "Where were you?"

Mathilda ignored their questions. "Where are you going with your machine?" she asked simply.

"Just across to the market," Timmy replied in a strained voice. The machine was getting heavy.

As they made it to the next landing, Timmy smiled disarmingly. "Well, we're sure glad you're back, wherever you were. Now you can sneak us pastries when your dad's not looking."

Mathilda made as if to giggle, but the strangest thing happened: although her mouth seemed to laugh, not a single sound came out. She just stood there with an odd grin that was most peculiar.

Timmy had never seen anything like it and was a little taken aback. Mathilda skipped away.

When they stepped out onto the busy street, it was already late in the afternoon, and long shadows stretched across the road. It was rush hour in Elyzandrium, and the street was clogged with bicycles and vehicles of all sorts. Some flying machines hovered overhead. Humans and animals alike walked past the boys, gaping in wonder at the wooden apparatus. It had pulleys and levers, and intricate mechanized arms of all shapes and sizes. The boys carefully put their invention down so they could take a quick rest. Timmy eyed his friends.

"Catch your breath, lads. But we better hurry. It's already late, and the fruit market might close soon."

"What do you think he'll pay for it?" Simon asked as he pulled out a hand mirror. He checked himself quickly to make sure his fur was in place.

"I reckon we'll have all the fruit we want for the rest of the year, as per my latest calculation," Jasper said with a big smile.

Casper quickly pulled out a notepad and scribbled something.

"Actually, that's not quite right," he countered his brother, squinting. "If we manage to haggle a bit,

we should be able to get some cashew nuts in the deal."

Simon smiled a big smile, showing off his perfect teeth. "I *do* love cashew nuts."

Jasper eyed Casper spitefully, holding out his own notepad. "That's incorrect. Look at this algorithm. If anything, it will be almonds. Look."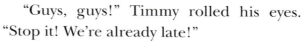

"Cashews," Casper insisted.

"Almonds!" Jasper said angrily.

With that, the two piglet brothers jumped on each other. Notepads flying, they rolled around in the street.

"Guys, guys!" Timmy rolled his eyes. "Stop it! We're already late!"

After a moment, he managed to break them apart.

"Cashews or almonds, both sound quite nice! C'mon, guys. No time to quarrel."

They walked on.

Sweaty and tired, the friends slowly lowered the machine onto the dusty cobblestones. Simon, not surprisingly, took the opportunity to polish his fur, making sure it was as shiny as ever. The others caught their breath. They still had a long way to go.

Timmy recognized where they were. He had an idea.

"Guys, I know a shortcut. If we cut through the alley-ways, we'll save quite a bit of time."

He nodded toward the alley ahead. Its narrow opening looked dark.

"You know as well as I do that that would be risky," Simon protested. "Let's face it, I don't want to turn into anyone's afternoon snack if we come across the wrong crowd. Didn't you learn anything on the streets? Predators could be anywhere."

"Yeah, Timmy. I don't know . . . ," Casper said nervously. "It'll be dark soon, and, well . . . we're just a bunch of inventors . . . geeks, really. Not tough at all."

They all knew that was pretty much true.

"But it'll take longer to go back the regular way," Timmy argued. He knew that taking the alley probably wasn't a great idea, but he also really, really wanted to sell this machine today. Free fruit for a year! And maybe cashews or almonds too! And there were four of them, quick-minded and inventive. What was the worst that could happen?

Jasper started a quick calculation in his mind.

"Based on current parameters, the risk will be about point four on the Riskman scale."

"Point three, actually . . . ," Casper began.

Jasper darkened and was about to pull out his notepad. Timmy sighed.

"That doesn't sound so bad! C'mon, lads. We'll be through there in a flash."

Under Timmy's guidance, they maneuvered through the winding alleys, stumbling in the darkness under the weight of the orange-peeling machine.

Soon the alleys grew narrower, and the noise of the main street faded. Only a sliver of darkening blue sky could be seen far above them. The houses grew shoddier and shoddier. Still, the boys pushed on. Simon lost track of how many turns they had made; he hoped Timmy knew what he was doing. Then he thought of something.

"Hold on just one second." Simon peered over at the others. "Isn't the Riskman scale used to measure radioactivity? You know, the winds and colors and all that? I think I read that in a nature magazine once."

That was when a large, dark shadow fell over the four friends. They all stopped and looked up.

"You think you're so smart, eh?" came a gruff voice. "But you're just a pack of nerds. And you're a long way from home."

In front of them, blocking their path, stood one of the Gribble cousins. The Gribbles were wild boars. They were tall, broad, and thick-necked. As far as Timmy had heard, they had always been bad kids, none too intelligent, but what they lacked above the

shoulders they made up for in muscle. Nobody knew exactly how many of them there were, because they all looked pretty much alike. Timmy had heard there were anywhere from four to as many as twelve. They were infamous for stealing things. Some even said they had kidnapped little children—humans and animals— although Timmy couldn't imagine why anyone would do such a monstrous thing.

Two of them now came up from behind the boys, blocking any chance for escape.

"What you got there?" the biggest one said.

"Looks like something we need," another one said.

"It's nothing," Timmy managed to squeak. "Nothing of any value whatsoever."

"Then you don't mind if we take it, do you?"

Timmy tried to be brave.

"Actually, we do mind." He held up a finger. "It wouldn't be right, you see. We built it, and it's not for you to take."

"Hey now, listen to this one."

The cousins laughed.

"You've got guts, little guy. But step aside and let us take what is rightfully yours," the biggest cousin said in a mocking tone.

More laughter.

The friends knew all was lost. They just stood there for a moment, desperately exchanging glances, not sure what to do. Two more Gribble cousins came from the shadows.

They were surrounded.

Jasper and Casper were the first to buckle. They dropped their end of the machine, and it slammed to the ground. The brothers bolted into a small doorway, too quickly for the big boars to react.

Still holding up the other end, Timmy looked at Simon. Their eyes met in silent agreement. The next second, Simon darted sideways, managing to squeeze by two of the cousins. Timmy tried to follow, but one of the Gribbles stepped forward and blocked his path. He spun back around, his cat reflexes working overtime. Two of the boars flailed their huge arms at him. He was cornered.

"Get him!"

Suddenly Timmy leapt. He managed to grab a hold of a window-sill and hauled himself over the edge, then quickly clawed his way up the house's façade, finding cracks and holes to grab on to.

The Gribbles scrambled over and swatted at him. "Come down here! We're not finished with you!" they bellowed.

He climbed higher, looking down

at the furious boars trying to scale the wall below him. They immediately slid down again. Being so big and thick-necked, they were horrible climbers.

Finally Timmy reached the rooftop and slung himself over the edge. He could hear the Gribble cousins stomping around and yelling as he ran as fast as he could. He skipped across roofs, hopped over chimneys, and jumped over more alleyways. Timmy ran and ran. He didn't stop until he was absolutely sure the Gribble cousins were far, far away.

Simon, Jasper, and Casper had all run into the same building. Having scrambled up and down stairs, through living rooms and kitchens (one with a very surprised goose family having dinner), back across alleys, and through more doorways, they now stood huddled together on one of the main streets. They were out of breath, and shaking from the adrenaline rush. Simon looked back.

"Where's Timmy?"

"Thought he was with you," Casper answered, still catching his breath.

"He was right behind us." Jasper peered into the darkness of the alley. "He's not coming."

All three squinted into the gloom. Nobody wanted to go back in there, not with the Gribbles still running around. Simon knew his best friend, though.

"He'll be okay. He *has* to be okay. It's Timmy. He always finds a way."

The three friends looked at each other, help-less. Sullenly they started through the streets toward the bakery.

Chapter 2

NIGHT HAD FALLEN, and a giant yellow moon hung over the rooftops. Timmy, still sitting on a shingled roof, peered down at the streets. He was lost, that much he knew. He was also exhausted, and getting cold, and homesick. Carefully, using a fire escape, he made his way down to a side street that didn't look too dark.

The street was empty. Red lanterns were hung between buildings, and through an unlit window a solemn song was playing on someone's record player. Timmy picked a direction at random. This was a part of Elyzandrium he had never been to before. The houses seemed older. In fact, they were much more charming than the buildings in his part of town.

He saw a couple coming toward him, locked in an embrace. Timmy tried to get their attention, but they were too caught up in being in love.

Oh shucks, he thought. He was a little embarrassed

to admit it, but he wanted to be in love too, not lost and lonely and cold. Those stupid Gribbles. If he ever saw them again, he was going to whoop their behinds, he promised himself. Not that he had any idea how to do that.

Timmy felt drowsy, and the cold gripped him now. It was terribly late, and he was awfully hungry. He saw a group of city guards farther ahead. He didn't want to get into any more trouble than he was in already, so he darted down another street.

A light drizzle began to fall. It was chilly, and the mist made the streetlights glow softly. Timmy shivered. He hated the rain. (He was a cat, after all.) There was no good place to take cover, so he found a pile of boxes stacked along one of the houses and sank down behind them. He tried his best to arrange them in a way that would shield him from the rain. Finally he rested his little head against one of them and fell asleep.

Across town, in a tall, dark building, a strange, enormous blue rabbit stood and looked out from a balcony. The nighttime view was spectacular. The city below him looked like a glowing sea of lights. Rabbit was very happy to be back here. It had been too long. He remembered having to flee this place—the place of his birth, as he liked to think of it—many years before. Since then, he had gathered his riches in the most remote corners of the world. Now he was back, and nobody seemed to remember him. And that, he thought, suited his plan just perfectly. This was where he would be born again, where he would finally gain what he had longed for: A real soul. Real life.

Rabbit was very tall for a rabbit. Quite large across his belly too. He thought that was fitting for someone of his stature. His long ears stood straight up almost all the time. He wore a long black coat, which had been made by the best tailors west of the Black

Mountains. It reached almost all the way to the floor. Shifty crimson eyes sat like little buttons in his head, and his face was stiff and expressionless, like that of a robot. The most striking thing about him, though, was his brilliant blue fur. He had never really reflected on why his fur was blue, but he rather liked it that way.

He was just about to go into his sleeping quarters when there was a hesitant knock on the door. He knew who it would be.

"Come in," he said impatiently. His voice sounded hollow.

The door swung open, and two of the Gribble cousins came in. Between them, they were carrying the stolen orange-peeling machine.

"Hi, boss."

"What's this?"

"Dunno, but thought you might like it. You know, maybe as parts for your own machine," the larger cousin said. "What's your machine for, anyway?"

"Put it down over there." Rabbit pointed to a corner, ignoring the question. "And don't touch anything."

"Sure, boss."

The cousins carried the contraption to the corner, careful not to knock over any of the strange-looking equipment in the large room. Then the bigger cousin, whose name was Dobie, straightened his back and looked over at his boss. "Anything else you need?" He sounded a little scared.

Rabbit looked at him blankly. "Out. Get out. I will call on you when I need you. Don't try to think for yourself. You will just hurt that thick head of yours."

"Okay, boss. Sorry, boss."

Dobie and his cousin bowed their heads and made their way out.

Timmy felt himself being shaken awake. Confused, he looked up, rubbing the sleep out of his eyes. He started to make out the large, dark silhouettes of five city guards above him. They were staring at him, and they did not look pleased.

"There's no sleeping in the street," one of them said. He was obviously the leader, with fancy shoulder pads and a tall helmet. "Move along. Go home."

Timmy slowly got up, shivering against the cold.

"He's a kitten. Shouldn't be in this part of town," someone said.

"Yeah, he's probably a troublemaker," a third guard said. "A thief, maybe. Part of a gang, I figure."

The leader looked grimly down at little Timmy.

"You got a name, kitten?"

Timmy looked up at the sullen guards.

"Timmy."

"Well, Timmy. What're you up to in this part of town

anyhow, huh? You'll be coming with us. There's a nice piece of floor for you to sleep on in jail until we find your parents."

"But can't I just go home? Like you said at first. Remember? I promise I'll go straight home."

Timmy looked at the big guard with pleading eyes. For a split second, he thought the guard might let him go. Then the guard's face turned stern again.

"If we let all criminals go, this town would be a circus."

With that, he picked Timmy up by his nape. He was about to toss him into a sack that the guard behind him was holding open when they heard a voice behind them.

"Excuse me." The voice had authority.

The guards spun around.

An old, rather rotund man dressed in an extravagantly patterned overcoat stepped up to them through the mist. His face was round and friendly, with an impossibly long, thin beard that snaked down from his chin. A pair of round spectacles sat on his big nose.

"Is everything as it should be over here?" the man continued.

"Mind your own business, old man," the lead guard sneered.

"Oh my. How rude."

The old man withdrew something from his big coat.

He held it up in front of him. The guards, surprised, looked at it. It looked like a little toy dragonfly made of metal and wood, with thin paper wings.

"Sir, you better put that away, or we—"

Suddenly the toy started glowing and buzzing, and to the guards' surprise, it took flight. It swooped around them, glowing with purple light, leaving a faint trail of sparkles. The guards stopped, completely mesmerized by the strange flying object. Big smiles soon spread across their faces, and they started to giggle like children.

"There, there," the old man said soothingly.

The guards' spears fell to the ground. They did little pirouettes, all the while trying to keep the dragonfly in their sight. Timmy momentarily looked on in amazement, then saw his chance and carefully snuck around the dancing men. He walked up to the bearded man, who gazed down at him through his round spectacles.

"It's a magical toy," he explained matter-of-factly. "It makes people joyous."

Timmy was grateful to the man for getting him out of this trouble, but he was also a little suspicious.

"Did you make it?"

"I did indeed. I'm a toymaker. My name is Alfred. Alfred the toymaker."

"I'm Timmy. I'm an inventor."

"Well, Timmy, it seemed like you needed a bit of help. You're a long way from home, aren't you?" His tone was gracious and sincere.

"Thank you, kind sir. Yes, I'm a bit lost, I suppose."

Alfred smiled. Next to them, the soldiers were giggling and playing hopscotch. Timmy thought the entire thing absurd.

"Now then. It's quite late," Alfred said. "Why don't you come have a cup of tea with me in my shop? And perhaps some cookies? You must be hungry. I have a back room where you can sleep a bit more too."

Timmy wasn't sure. Should he trust this stranger?

He looked around the deserted street. A cold fog was slowly rolling in, and he shivered slightly. His day had already gone as badly as it could, he figured. And this man had gone out of his way to help him.

"A cup of tea would be quite nice."

"Very well. It's settled, then. My shop isn't far."

With that, the two started down the street. Timmy turned around one last time. Through the fog he could still see the soldiers. They were playing tag. He giggled.

Chapter 3

ALFRED PUSHED OPEN a heavy wooden door, revealing a small, dark room. He shuffled inside and lit a small oil lamp.

"Please come in, Timmy."

Timmy timidly stepped inside. The warm glow of the oil lamp lit up a space that took his breath away. On every shelf and table (and there were many of them) stood the most wonderful toys Timmy could ever have dreamt of. Some were big, others small. Some looked like intricate machines, and others were just simple shapes. As he walked around in amazed silence, the toymaker regarded him ruefully.

"They're wonderful. Just wonderful" was all Timmy could think to say. "Did you make them?"

"Not all of them. Some were made a long time ago by my father and grandfather. And my grandfather's father too, I suppose."

"Alfred . . . are all these toys magical, like that

dragonfly?" Timmy asked. He was as nervous as he was excited.

Alfred took a deep breath. "Most of them. And some of them have a magic that you would barely notice. Unless you knew exactly what to look for."

Timmy didn't know what that meant, but before he could ask, Alfred disappeared into a small kitchen area. Timmy could hear the clinking sound of teacups being taken from their cabinet. A minute later, Alfred returned with a large tray holding not only a teapot and cups but also a huge plate piled high with pastries and cakes.

"Come, we'll take the tea in my workroom."

He led Timmy through a maze of little rooms. It reminded Timmy of the alleys earlier that day, but this time he didn't feel unsafe.

"This is where I create my toys," Alfred announced. They had reached a large room filled with vials and glass globes containing all kinds of strange liquids and powders. The room looked like a laboratory. A very strange but wonderful laboratory, Timmy thought.

Alfred cleared off a small table and set down the tray. He poured the tea and offered a cup to Timmy. Timmy carefully sipped the hot liquid; it tasted of mint and spices. The toymaker studied his guest curiously.

"Do you like it?"

"Yes, it's quite nice." Timmy took another sip.

"So? Had a rough day?" Alfred inquired.

"A bit rough, I suppose. . . . It was all going well, until . . . Well, it was my fault. I tried to take a shortcut, and the Gribble cousins . . . suddenly they were just there. And they stole our orange-peeling machine that we had just finished."

The toymaker nodded slowly.

"The Gribbles . . ." Alfred looked as though the name meant something to him, and as if he was going to comment on it, but instead he poured some more tea and started telling Timmy of his many years in the shop.

"You see, this shop has belonged to my family for as long as anyone in Elyzandrium can remember." Alfred's face glowed in the warmth of a kerosene lantern while he talked, and his smile was broad.

They drank more tea, and Timmy began telling a little about himself.

"I grew up in an orphanage, and that's where I met my best friend, Simon. Neither he nor I liked it much; the people who ran it were very mean. So we managed to escape."

"Where did you live after that?" Alfred said, peering over his teacup.

"On the streets. It was tough, but we managed. We started inventing things, and people wanted to buy what we built."

Timmy sipped his tea and continued. He told Alfred that he had heard rumors that his mother belonged to one of Elyzandrium's finest families and that his father was an alley cat.

"But I have no idea where they are today. In the alleys there was this old-timer, Vince, who always seemed to keep an eye out for me. I often wondered if he could be my dad, but he never said anything, and I never dared to ask."

Alfred saw longing in Timmy's eyes, but also a quiet strength.

"Now I have my friends," Timmy continued. "They are my family. Our invention business is really taking off, you know. I guess I'm pretty happy."

Timmy began to get sleepy. It was very late, and his eyelids were drooping. He listened some more to Alfred's stories and soon curled up into a little ball and fell asleep. He dreamt of the toys that night, how they suddenly came alive and Timmy was in the middle of all of them, conducting them as though they were a symphony orchestra. The toys and Timmy played, jumped, and laughed together.

Timmy woke with a start the following morning and found he was tucked under a blanket. He looked around, confused at first, squinting his large yellow eyes at the strange new surroundings. The pale morning light made the toys look even more impressive, and everything that had happened the night before streamed back into his mind. *What a strange turn of events,* he thought.

He got up, stretched out his hind legs, and shifted his ears toward a tinkering sound in the next room. He walked softly in the direction of the sound.

As he entered the room, he saw that Alfred was sitting at his workbench, hunched over a minuscule object.

His stubby fingers were assembling something that resembled a mechanical spider. A new toy. He looked up at Timmy.

"Well, good morning, young sir. Sleep well?"

"Yes. I had the most wonderful dreams."

"Of the toys?" Alfred asked in a hopeful voice.

Timmy nodded. "They all came alive, wanting to play with me. And it was as if I could speak to them. Not with my voice but with my mind."

"Hmm . . . how very wonderful." Alfred raised his eyebrows in thought. "They do have that effect on you," he said after a moment. In fact, that wasn't true at all. Alfred knew full well that those dreams happened very, very rarely. To the chosen few. This little cat was very special indeed.

Timmy leapt up to the table. Alfred wound a small widget, and the spider started to move across the table,

lifting its long spindly legs over the surface. Timmy watched it with fascination. Alfred saw the sparkle of wonder in Timmy's eye. But he also recognized a curious understanding and an unmistakable empathy.

"I can teach you how to make some of this stuff, if you're interested," Alfred said.

"Teach me? Really?"

"Yes. But you would need to be patient."

"I could be patient," Timmy mumbled softly.

"Good. Well, the first thing you have to do is find the magical ingredients."

"Ingredients?"

"Sure. Magic doesn't come out of thin air, you know."

Timmy had never thought about it before, but he guessed that made sense. Then he thought of his friends, that they might be worried about him.

"My friends must be waiting for me."

"It won't take long," Alfred said kindly.

"I suppose they could wait just a little longer."

"Then let's go right away."

"What kind of ingredients?"

"Come. You will see."

Chapter 4

ALFRED SLUNG A leather bag over his shoulder and motioned for Timmy to follow. He led Timmy down an old corridor.

The room at the end was filled to the brim with discarded experiments and odd-looking pieces of scientific equipment. Behind the rubble was a small iron door. The toymaker unlocked it, lit an old kerosene lantern, and pulled the heavy door open. It gave a dull squeak.

The air smelled stale and musty as Timmy peered into the thick blackness. Holding the lantern high, Alfred spoke calmly while feeling his way along a stone tunnel.

"This tunnel is many centuries old. Nobody knows who built it. It was a stroke of luck that my great-grandfather's great-grandfather found it."

Within a few minutes, Timmy's eyes had adjusted somewhat. He wondered what could possibly be at the other end.

"This way." The toymaker held the lantern toward a steep staircase. He led the way down the slippery steps. The rough stone walls glittered with minerals. The air smelled of damp earth, and there was also a strange sweet smell that Timmy couldn't quite place wafting up from below.

They seemed to descend for hours. Timmy stepped carefully, so as not to slip, and held on to the walls with

his paws. Alfred's large back bobbed side to side as he continued ever downward.

A faint blue glow emanated from below. It grew stronger, and suddenly the steps ended. Timmy looked around. To his surprise, they stood in a vast underground cavern. Giant stalactites and stalagmites loomed around them, and hundreds more, in all shapes and sizes, could be seen in the distance. He realized now that the blue glow came from tiny plants that grew all over the rocks. They looked like glow-in-the-dark pinpricks. Some were blue; others were green and purple and orange and yellow. Some were like lichen; others were in the shapes of little mushrooms or flowers. The scene looked truly magical.

Slowly Alfred moved forward, careful not to step on the glowing plant life.

Timmy felt as if he were an explorer on a strange planet. Alfred looked back, making sure he was keeping up.

Suddenly there was a swooshing sound, and Timmy felt something fly by right next to his head. He dove for cover. Alfred burst into a giggle.

"What was that?" Timmy exclaimed.

"Bats!" Alfred said, chuckling now. "Quite harmless, but they do have a knack for scaring you silly if you aren't paying attention."

With his pride only a little bit ruffled, Timmy got up again.

"I saw him coming a mile away. I was just testing my reflexes," he mumbled.

Alfred smiled and said nothing more on the matter. He pointed ahead and started walking again.

Every now and then, Alfred would lean down and pick a few of the flowers or mushrooms. He placed them carefully in one of the different compartments in the heavy leather bag over his shoulder. He explained how mixing the different species, in just the right amounts, in just the right order, and at just the right temperature, would make lights or sounds, or create illusions, and some of them would have magical effects.

"Many years ago," Alfred began, "when I was just a little boy, my father brought me down here. He taught me how to make magical toys with the help of these plants, just as his own father had once taught him. For years I studied the ways of mixing and blending, and extracting just the right amount of juice out of a leaf, or grinding seeds together and blending them with other extracts at the right temperature. It was knowledge that only my family had."

He grew quiet as they came to a serene lake. The water was very still and as black as night. There was a rowboat pulled up on the shore. Alfred pushed it into the water, and they climbed in.

Alfred rowed silently, dipping the oars into the dark water as carefully as he could. Timmy climbed to the front and looked down. He could see movement deep under the surface—something pale slithering through the waters.

He glanced back with a concerned look on his face.

"Very old creatures. Don't disturb them," Alfred whispered.

Timmy and Alfred finally reached the other shore, pulled the boat onto land, and continued on. The stone structures on this side were even more fantastic. There were deep ravines, falling into the blackest of

black. At other parts of the cave, the ceiling soared higher than Timmy could see.

At one point, Alfred stopped and threw his arms out with a high-pitched yell. Timmy's cat instincts were on such high alert, he almost dove to the ground for a second time; then he realized that the toymaker's outburst was one of joy. Alfred pointed excitedly. On the rock wall high above them grew some beautiful blue flowers.

"*Eufsporia galitinos marillimus*," Alfred explained. "Very rare . . . very rare indeed!" He shook little Timmy happily. "You bring good luck, don't you? This is a real treat." He craned his neck to look up. "It's just a shame they're so high up there."

He peered at Timmy.

"Cats are supposed to be good at climbing, aren't they?"

"I suppose."

"Do you think you could climb up there and pick a couple of those? Only the biggest ones; we need to let the smaller ones grow."

Timmy looked up. He thought they were awfully high, but feeling gratitude toward the old man, and having his pride to uphold, he knew he had to give it a go.

"Okay. Sure thing. No problemo."

He looked up again. He could do this, he decided.

Feeling intrepid, he started to climb. It was dark and slippery, but he soon found his footing in the little cracks and crannies. It was only when he looked down that he realized how far up he was. Fear gripped his gut momentarily, but he took a deep breath and brushed it away.

Up and up he went, and finally he was within a paw's grasp of the flowers. He reached out.

Just as he was about to take the biggest one, he could feel the fur on his nape stand straight up. In the shadows above, it was as if the air fluttered and moved.

Hundreds, if not thousands, of bats descended from the darkness and enveloped him. He could feel their leathery wings flapping against his fur and face. Their shrieks howled into his sensitive ears. He closed his eyes, but that just made it worse. Panicked, he could feel his grasp begin to slip. He opened his eyes again and looked around frantically, but all he could see was flapping gray-black bat wings and bat eyes and bat mouths. It was as if the air around him were boiling. His paws slipped away from the wall, and he fell.

As it was, being a cat did have its advantages. Timmy knew (he had time to reflect on this while he fell) that he had probably used up about three of his nine lives so far, but that still left six. With a little luck, perhaps those six would be enough to get him out of this mess. As Alfred would tell him later, it ended up being more like two. Yes, he hit his head against the rock, and his back, and his sensitive belly, but he also showed some amazing agility. He managed to slow his fall a little by grabbing on to tiny sections of rock when he could, and by flailing and waving his arms as he slid, so that at the end, when he hit the bottom, only two more of his lives had been used up.

Alfred rushed over to him, fearing the worst, but he cried out with happiness as little Timmy opened his eyes.

Then, to Alfred's even greater amazement, Timmy opened his left paw. And there, between his kitten claws, was one of the bright blue flowers.

"Oh joy! Oh dear! Oh my goodness! Alfred was beside himself with all kinds of emotion.

Timmy licked his scratches, smiled broadly at Alfred as he handed him the flower, and said, "Sorry I could only get you one."

"Timmy, you were brilliant." Alfred beamed.

Back up in the safety of the toy shop, Timmy sat in front of their loot. Alfred shook his head in bewilderment.

"Timmy, do you realize we now have ingredients

for hundreds of new magical toys?" He was most pleased—no, not pleased, ecstatic—over the blue flower that Timmy had collected, the rare *Eufsporia galitinos marillimus.*

Timmy looked at it; to him it looked like just a normal flower. But Alfred sat in front of it in wonder, slowly shaking his head and tearing up with happiness.

"Only once before in my long life have I been able to find this rare flower, and that was almost forty years ago."

"What did you use it for?"

Alfred grew quiet. "It doesn't matter. Now I am wiser and will prepare it with a thousand times more care."

He looked at Timmy. His heart was heavy with regret when he thought of what had happened when he had last prepared the *Eufsporia galitinos marillimus,* so many years ago. If only he had known back then what he knew now, he could have controlled the powerful magic within the blue petals. Instead . . . he had created something monstrous. Would he ever get the chance to correct his mistake?

He wondered if it was fate that had brought Timmy to him. Perhaps there was a reason why they had met.

Outside, a heavy rain hammered the glass windows, and thunder rolled in the distance. Timmy wondered how his life had changed so dramatically in just a day, how he could have made such an amazing new friend. He also wondered how Simon, Jasper, and Casper were doing. He hadn't seen them since the afternoon of the previous day. They must have been quite worried about him by now. Perhaps they too had gotten lost. He would have to go find them the next day.

Chapter 5

THE NEXT AFTERNOON, Timmy, Alfred, Simon, Jasper, and Casper found themselves talking and drinking tea together in the back of the toymaker's shop. Timmy wondered if Alfred ever drank anything besides tea, but he was a little afraid to ask.

Earlier that morning, Timmy and Alfred had paced the streets to find Timmy's three friends. Sure enough, they had found them up in the loft where our story began.

They had been very happy indeed to see Timmy again, and had been ever so grateful to Alfred for saving him from the guards and giving him food and shelter.

"We were so worried about you, Timmy," said Jasper.

"But we also knew you could take care of yourself," added Casper.

Simon had been particularly worried and had waited

in the loft for more hours than he could count. So long, in fact, that he had missed his date that evening with a particularly cute squirrel girl.

Now they sipped some of the spicy, hot tea, and Timmy told his friends of his previous day's adventure in the cave. They were all very curious about the magical toys—how they worked, and how the ingredients were mixed to make them, and who Alfred made them for, and what happened when the toys broke.

Spellbound and round-eyed, they listened when Alfred patiently answered even the most ridiculous questions. He let them play with a few of the toys, and they laughed and chased each other around and were just like inventors were supposed to be.

As they quieted down, Simon cleared his throat a bit nervously.

When all eyes were on him attentively, he asked: "Remember how two days ago this weird thing happened where it seemed like Mathilda couldn't laugh?

Well, it turns out she still can't laugh. So I asked her father down at the bakery, and he said that Mathilda had been missing for a few days, and he and his wife had been terribly worried. Then he had found her sitting in front of the bakery one morning, looking rather confused. Mathilda herself had no memory of the missing days. For her, it was just a vague blur, but she soon realized that she couldn't laugh anymore."

They had met several other kids, both animals and

humans, who were just like Mathilda. Simon loved to tell jokes (in fact, he took pride in inventing new jokes and considered himself quite a funny mink) and would tell them to any kid he encountered. It had happened five or six times, just in their neighborhood, that the children had stood there with their mouths open as if they were laughing at Simon's jokes, but not a sound would come out. It was the strangest thing. And they too had been missing for a few days, then simply turned up again.

On top of that, Simon had heard that the Gribble

cousins were continuing their troublemaking through-out the streets and alleyways of Elyzandrium. They had even been seen with a biker gang that rode around on steam-powered motorcycles, and all the bikers were iguanas. Iguanas! This sounded pretty ridiculous to all of them.

Timmy was shocked. Their city had always been so peaceful. Now both people and animals had to be fearful of these criminal gangs, even in the middle of the day.

His head sank, and he propped it up again with his paws. He looked at his friends. He looked at Al-fred. He looked at all the wonderful magical toys around him.

"This is our city," he said. "We were all born here. It

used to be quite nice, and now it's being run by gangs. Something has to be done," he declared. "It's one thing to steal our orange-peeling machine and chase us all across the city, but it's another thing to be intimidating people all over town. And small children, at that! And for all we know, the Gribbles are behind all the children losing their ability to laugh too. No, this won't do at all, guys."

For a moment, the room was silent. Alfred regarded the group of friends solemnly. Simon looked at Timmy. Timmy let his gaze travel over Jasper and Casper. In turn, the brothers looked back at Alfred. Finally Timmy spoke up again.

"I, for one, will not sit idly by while this is going on. I refuse to be a victim. We will fight back. Our orange-peeling machine is probably long gone, sold for lots of money, but that won't stop me from standing up for others who may have the same thing befall them."

The friends nodded. Timmy liked how he had used the word "befall." It had sounded important. He continued.

"We could fight back. We have everything we need right here, in this toy shop. I've seen what these toys can do. If Alfred can help us create some magical tools, we can do anything. We can form our own gang—like . . . a ninja gang! We'd stand up to the Gribbles or anyone else who wreaks havoc on our town. Enough is enough. Who's with me?"

Timmy wasn't sure where he'd gotten "ninjas" from, but he thought it sounded good. And he actually believed in what he was saying. He repeated the last sentence louder.

"Who's with me?"

The friends all looked at each other.

"I am!" Simon was the first. Then Jasper and Casper joined in.

"And we are!" they exclaimed simultaneously.

Timmy looked to Alfred. "Will the toymaker help us with this quest? Will he make magical gear for us, so that we can put an end to this suffering?"

Alfred studied the group. One kitten, one mink, and two rather plump piglets who were good at math. His eyes were serious. At last he spoke.

"I will. Indeed I will. We'll work together. And you can all stay here in the shop while we figure out our plan."

Chapter 6

THERE WAS MUCH planning to be done. The four friends were about to set out on their first mission. Alfred had shown them some basics about how his magic worked and had constructed a special device for each of them.

For Jasper and Casper, he had made shoes that enabled them to jump really far, and even float in the air for a while. They looked a little like metal clogs but had intricate machinery inside. Both of the brothers immediately tried to calculate the aerodynamics that made the shoes work, but neither of them could quite figure it out.

Simon got a pair of goggles. They were clunky and heavy, and at first he didn't like them one bit.

"They don't really go with my look," he said. But when Alfred hit a switch on the side, Simon jumped with excitement. "I can see through the wall!" he cried. "Jeez, Alfred. You sure have a lot of clutter behind that closet door." Alfred blushed, but they all laughed. Simon was so excited that he forgot about the goggles' unfashionable appearance.

And finally, for Timmy, Alfred had constructed a very special walking stick. It looked just like a normal walking stick, but it could open and transform into all kinds of useful things. When thrown, it would always come back to the hands of the one who had thrown it. It could grow to about ten times its original length. These were only a few of the things it could do; not even Alfred knew all its capabilities.

Alfred, with design input from Simon, had also made outfits for each of them, all in black, complete with belts. Simon had then added a final touch: black headbands. After they put their new outfits on, they looked at each other and thought they all looked quite cool. And quite appropriately, Timmy thought, like a band of little ninjas. Alfred came into the room.

"Well, look at you!" he exclaimed. "Not bad at all. Quite the fearsome troop. Heroes all!"

"Yes, I think our outfits are pretty awesome. And our magical gear is great. All thanks to you, Alfred," Timmy said.

"No, my young friend. Thanks to *you*. This was all your idea. I just sat there and listened, remember?"

Timmy knew that was true, but he didn't feel entirely comfortable with being the one who'd started a ninja crime-fighting gang. It wasn't like anything he'd ever done before. It was just that he didn't like being bullied or stolen from. And the four friends were a good gang. Alfred stepped away.

Simon came up to Timmy.

"Okay, you old street cat. Let's see what trouble we can get into. I hope we didn't get dressed up for nothing."

Simon put on his own headband and paraded in front of a mirror, striking fearsome ninja poses and practicing a mean glare to use on the Gribbles.

Timmy smiled at his friends.

"Okay, lads. Let's go fight some crime!"

An hour later, they moved single file across a high rooftop. They looked out over their city as they walked toward the same dark alleys where they had first been attacked. The tall bamboo skyscrapers glittered like rocket ships in the distance, white smoke rose from steam engines and chimneys below, and lonely flying balloons drifted slowly across the blue night. At first, they felt self-conscious, but they felt better when they started complimenting themselves on their ultra-cool ninja outfits. Simon looked particularly sharp, as usual. Jasper's and Casper's clogs clinked a little as they moved. Timmy held his magical cane tightly.

They reached the right neighborhood and stalked across the rooftops, spying on the alleys below. They peered down, seeing if they could spot the Gribbles or any other troublemakers. Everything seemed calm—no sign of the wild boar cousins—but then . . .

It was Simon who saw it first, using his fancy goggles. A flying machine, maybe two hundred yards away, was in trouble. It was way too low. The engine sputtered, and the wings dipped sharply left, then right. He pointed:

"Look! It's gonna crash!"

They watched it slowly spiral downward; the pilot seemed to struggle to gain altitude. Timmy quickly calculated where it might land and started running. The others followed, and the group sprang from building to building. With their magical clogs, Jasper and Casper could bounce far ahead.

The winged machine dropped down between two tall buildings and out of sight. There was a hollow bang, then a metallic scraping sound, then silence.

When Timmy reached the narrow street, he heard yelling through the blinding dust and smoke. It sounded shrill and angry.

In the pilot's seat was a cat. She was yelling loudly and furiously, flailing her arms, pushing poor Casper away.

"Can't a girl land her plane without being attacked? Get away from me!"

Casper backed away from the cat, turning to the others with a defeated look. Timmy stepped up and straightened his back. He tried to use his most heroic voice.

"We are here to rescue you. Stay calm."

"Rescue me! I'm in no need of rescuing, especially from a bunch of . . . of . . . *bandits* like yourselves!"

Timmy was stunned at this outburst but could understand how she might mistake their ninja clothing for that of, well, bandits.

The girl hopped out of the cockpit and took off her goggles. As she did so, Timmy was overwhelmed. This scowling cat was the toughest and coolest and most beautiful cat girl he had ever seen. Simon noticed it too, and struck a pose, about to pour on his usual charm. But Timmy wanted to be the one she talked to, and he quickly continued.

"We're not bandits; we're ninjas." He realized how silly it sounded as the words left his mouth.

Simon took a step back as Timmy spoke.

"Ehm . . . I mean, we're good ninjas, like the ones that save people and stuff."

"Good ninjas?" She started laughing.

"Yes, that's right. And we're here to save you after your crash."

"First of all, I was *landing*, not crashing. Okay, it was a hard and sudden landing, but a landing nonetheless.

Second, let me get this straight. Those are supposed to be ninja outfits? Are those headbands? And you just happened to be here, at this very spot, in case someone was about to crash—or, I mean, *land*—their flying machine?"

"Exactly like that, yes. Yes, that's it." Timmy looked foolishly at the others. "I'm Timmy, and this is Simon,

Jasper, and Casper." The others smiled and waved awkwardly.

"And aren't ninjas supposed to have swords or throwing stars and stuff like that?"

"We have other cool stuff. Much cooler stuff, actually."

She looked them over. "Yeah, nice stick."

Timmy looked at his stick. He hadn't yet quite figured out how to make it work.

"It's actually rather nice" was all he could muster.

The cat girl regarded the four friends for a moment, then looked at the dust settling around her flying machine. Her voice changed as she made an effort to sound at least a little polite.

"Well, it was nice meeting you ninja chaps, but I'm outta here. You all have a splendid evening now."

With that, she turned and started to walk away.

"Wait!" Timmy couldn't let her just go off like that.

"What?" She tried her best to sound annoyed, but Timmy could hear a hint of curiosity in her tone. That was enough for him.

"You have a name?"

"Flores. That's my name."

She had meant to just stay nonchalant and aloof. But this cat seemed quite harmless. Maybe he was even a cool cat after all. Well, maybe not cool, but kind of

cute. Well, maybe not cute, but interesting. In a silly
way. Especially with his headband.

"Well, Flores." Timmy felt his courage come back.
"We patrol the streets in this part of town, looking for
any thieves, bad street gangs, or troublemakers. If you
see any suspicious activity, can you let us know? We
hang out at the old toy shop, five or six blocks over."

Timmy tried to nod casually in the direction of
Alfred's shop. He made a mental note to reassess the
coolness factor of his outfit. Perhaps the headbands

hadn't been such a great idea. Still, he thought that maybe he had pulled off looking just a little like he actually knew what he was doing.

Flores smiled at him.

"All right, kids," she said. "I'll remember that until I forget it. You go play night watch, and maybe I'll see you when I see you."

She was too cool for school, this one, Timmy thought. Yet he liked her much more than he wanted to.

He watched her saunter off, leaving her machine parked in the street. When she was gone, he turned to the others.

"Well, kids, I reckon we've done all we can do tonight."

He tried to sound cool, but the others just smiled at him.

They started walking back through the streets. Timmy looked at his newly formed ninja gang, and although the evening had been a bit of a mess, he was still proud of them. And of himself. He wondered if he would ever see Flores again. What a girl!

Such a radical cat . . . quite the rebel, and oh so beautiful. She would never go for an inventor street cat like him. It was a ridiculous thought.

But now he was a *ninja* cat! And they had some truly radical gear! Magical, even! (Even if they hadn't really gotten to use the gear much.) His mind raced.

Simon came up alongside him. "You did all right," he said with a smile.

"With what?"

"What do you think? With the girl, stupid."

"I did? I thought I botched it pretty bad."

"Well, you botched it, all right, but somehow it worked for you. I notice these things. I'm actually a little proud of you."

"You are?"

"Yep. You have a long way to go before you're as smooth as I am, but it wasn't bad. For a cat, anyway."

Timmy was suddenly glad that his face was covered with fur, so Simon couldn't see him blushing. He smiled at his old friend. He knew it had taken a lot for Simon to admit that.

They walked in silence through the empty streets. But all the way back to the shop, Timmy kept thinking about Flores. He had never met anyone like her before, and he couldn't quite decide how he felt about her. Trying to be logical, he figured she might make a great addition to the gang, what with her flying machine and all. He even tried to introduce the idea to the others on the way, but they just laughed at him. They knew what was up.

Still, Timmy couldn't let go of the thought.

Chapter 7

OVER HOT TEA, they discussed the evening's events. It was already quite late, but Timmy wanted to go through it all while it was still fresh in their memories.

"It might be better to separate and patrol one block each so we could cover more ground," suggested Casper.

Simon objected. "We're much stronger together. We'd lose precious time if we were too spread out to hear each other."

Timmy agreed. Separating would work if they had something to communicate with, like a little device they could speak into that would let them hear each other's voices, but nothing like that had ever been invented.

So they all agreed that staying together was still the way to go. Jasper thought it would be good to get higher up so they could watch a bigger area. But how were they going to do that? Casper brought out his notepad and calculated that they could be 5.65 degrees Celsius more effective with a higher vantage point.

Of course Timmy thought of Flores's flying machine, which would be great to patrol with, but he didn't mention it because of how his friends had all laughed at the idea before. He thought the others would just assume that he'd brought it up because he liked her, and even though it was clear that she was tough and smart too, Timmy knew they were probably right. So he didn't say anything more.

Alfred sat listening to them talk. He would get up to make more tea and come back with a new pot, always with some freshly baked cookies to go with it.

In the end, they all agreed to pretty much stick to the plan. They would keep the nighttime patrols, stay together, pick a different section of town each night, and stay vigilant.

But they might lose the headbands.

It was three nights later that their new careers as crime fighters formally began. At sundown they set out, keeping to the rooftops and trying the best they could to stay out of sight. They would jump from building to building, or crawl along the steam pipes that lay across the roofs if the distance between buildings was too far to jump. Jasper and Casper had a good advantage and often took the lead, being able to jump long distances with their magic clogs.

This night started like the others. At first, nothing seemed out of the ordinary. They stopped on the roof of a café they all knew. Each one took a corner and watched for anything unusual.

Simon, with his goggles, suddenly looked around and motioned to the others. As they scurried over, he pointed toward the ground. And there, just at the next corner, stood an old dog. He was holding a large basket covered with a blanket. They all knew who the dog was: his name was Humphrey. He was a popular musician at the local restaurants and would often wander the streets with his ukulele, playing a song for anyone who would give him a penny.

"I can see five figures moving in on him," Simon said. He quickly let the others take peeks through his goggles. And indeed, when they could see through the buildings, they could see five rather large characters slowly sneaking up on poor old Humphrey.

"The Gribbles?" Timmy asked.

"Looks like it. Wonder what it is he's carrying. Must be something they want."

"Something they think they can sell," Casper added.

"I really hate the Gribbles," Jasper piped up.

"Let's move." Timmy hurried over to the edge of the building. The others followed. They had practiced this kind of scenario with Alfred's help, and everyone knew what to do. Using the fire escape, they quickly made their way down to the street and took their positions. Simon went left around the block, Jasper and Casper went right, and Timmy started moving up the middle, toward where they had seen Humphrey.

They were in the nick of time: they could hear old Humphrey suddenly start to howl and bark. Timmy was there first, as a ninja leader should be.

Indeed, it *was* the Gribbles. Humphrey was too old to try to run but was hanging on to his basket like it was worth its weight in gold. He was surrounded.

Timmy strode toward them, trying to appear confident. "Hey!" he shouted.

The second after he did so, he suddenly realized what a bad idea it had probably been. Who did he think he was? He was barely two feet tall, wearing a black outfit (still with his headband on) and carrying a walking stick. What could he possibly do?

These thoughts struck him all at once as he watched

the Gribble cousins turn in his direction and grin. Timmy was scared. Really scared. And he hated violence. Why not just talk out a problem? That seemed like the only way to solve it. Unfortunately, the Gribbles weren't much for talking. And even if he hated violence, he was about to step knee-deep into it, frightened beyond his wits.

But then he saw Humphrey's face, the poor old soul. He saw how relieved he was that anybody gave a hoot, that anybody would stand up for him. It gave Timmy strength, and it gave him the courage he needed.

It was clear that the Gribbles recognized him. The fear still darted around in his heart. But then he heard familiar voices from the left and right.

"Hey!" Simon yelled from the left.

"Hey!" Jasper and Casper shouted in unison from the right.

The momentary confusion that this generated in the Gribbles was enough for the four friends to gain the advantage.

The Gribbles were still more than twice as tall as any of them and probably outweighed them four to one. But none of that mattered.

As the cousins spun around, trying to figure out what was happening, Jasper and Casper had already leapt up into the air, and Simon was jumping and rolling straight into the middle. As for Timmy, he finally got a taste of what his magic cane was capable of.

It was as if it followed his thoughts. When he wanted it to be ten feet long, it was. When he wanted it to divide into four prongs, it did. When he wanted it to spin around like blades from one of the flying machines, it was already spinning. Timmy was amazed. Simon moved with the speed of lightning, striking with his made-up ninja poses. And he looked good doing it. He must have practiced in secret, Timmy

thought. Probably in front of a mirror. The Gribbles simply couldn't keep up.

Yes, there was some bruising going on, and yes, violence is a bad thing, and even the four friends got a few scrapes and bumps, but in the end the Gribbles decided that enough was enough and ran away for the first time in their lives.

As the blur of the fight subsided and Timmy was trying to get his breath back, good old Humphrey stood there in awe. He looked at Timmy and the others, and the expression in his eyes was enough to convey the gratitude he felt. But even so, he bowed his head to all of them.

"Thank you all. Where did you come from?"

Timmy pointed to the rooftops.

"We are going to make a change in this town." Timmy felt proud. "My name is Ninja Timmy, and this is my gang."

"Ninja Timmy?"

"That's right. Ninja Timmy. Spread the word."

"Aren't ninjas bad?"

"Well, we're good ninjas. With cooler gear than regular ninjas. Much cooler. Like this cane. Now spread the word."

Humphrey was a little confused but very grateful, so he let it go.

"Okay, I will. And thank you!"

He nodded to all of them. Humphrey was about to go, when Simon asked, "What were you carrying that they wanted so badly?"

"Oh, this?" Humphrey lifted the blanket from the basket. Inside, looking up with a yawn and a smile, was an adorable puppy.

"My son."

"Oh."

"I can't imagine why they would want him, though."

Timmy exchanged glances with the others. They could. Another attempted kidnapping. This was bad. Somebody was after the kids in this town.

Humphrey thanked them again, tipped his hat, and walked off down the street.

When he had left, Simon turned to Timmy:

"Ninja Timmy? And his gang? I thought we were doing this together!"

"Of course we are. I just . . . I don't know . . . wanted us to have a name. Like an official one."

"Well, think of another one. Perhaps one that includes *all* our names?"

"Timmy, Simon, Jasper, and Casper's Gang of Ninjas? That's awfully long and not very nice-sounding," Timmy objected.

"We can probably think of something better than that. And why would your name be first anyway? I am by far the handsomest member of this group, so if anyone should be the front figure, it should be me."

"Or," said Casper, "why not Casper, Jasper, Simon, and Timmy's Gang of Ninjas? I'm the smartest, so I should be first. . . ." At this, of course, Jasper jabbed him in the side, glared at him, and objected wildly that *he* was far smarter.

They argued like this all the way to the toy shop, and finally agreed that they would try to come up with a better name. But Simon and the others were still a little upset about the whole thing. It was a shame, because the night's mission had gone so perfectly. They had successfully stopped a crime and had chased off the big, bad Gribble cousins, their archenemies. Timmy thought it was pretty cool that they now had archenemies. Maybe even Flores would be impressed. He didn't quite know why it would be good to impress Flores, but he wanted to. He thought of her often and wondered if they'd ever see each other again.

Chapter 8

THE ANSWER TO that question came the next day. It was just before noon, and Timmy was still asleep in the back room at Alfred's toy shop. They had gotten back very late, and he was tired from the previous night's adventures. Alfred softly shook him awake. With a mumbled groan, Timmy turned away, pulling his blanket tight.

"Timmy, wake up. There's someone here asking for you," Alfred said.

"Who is it?" Timmy protested. He just wasn't ready to get up yet.

"Go see for yourself."

Still a little groggy, Timmy finally made himself get up. He stumbled, half-asleep, into the shop area. And there, standing with her back to him, looking at all the toys, was Flores. She turned around as he came in.

"Hey, there you are," she said.

"What's up?" Timmy tried to sound suave, swallowing his surprise.

"So is this your headquarters or what? Got some pretty rad stuff in here."

Timmy was quite astonished, and at the same time thrilled to see her.

"Thanks, but it's not our shop. We just hang out here. It belongs to Alfred, the toymaker."

"The old human dude?"

Timmy couldn't quite picture Alfred as a "dude," but he didn't want to argue about it.

"Yes."

Flores picked up one of the toys, studying it curiously.

"Be careful with that. It's magical."

"Magical? That's interesting." She put it down again. "So anyway, you mentioned that I should let you know if I saw anything suspicious in town. And, well, I have. I guess it's been going on for a while, but I've noticed it more lately."

"What's going on?"

"Kind of hard to explain, but it's all these kids. Both animal and human. They can't laugh anymore. They just kind of stand there with an odd grin when they're supposed to laugh. I know it sounds really weird, but I've never seen anything like it. I thought maybe you guys would like to know, being ninja crime fighters and all that."

Simon, Jasper, and Casper had now also come into the room, and Alfred hovered in the background. They looked at each other. Alfred stepped forward and spoke softly:

"I think we better have this conversation in the back."

They all followed Alfred into the room at the back of the shop. Sitting on boxes and on the workbenches, they gathered in a circle. Alfred spoke first.

"Flores, you're not the only one who's seen this happening. We've all noticed it, and we think it's getting worse. Can you tell us where these kids were?"

"This last time it was in the alleys behind the air-balloon station. And I also saw it in the ice cream shop on the main square."

Alfred shuffled over to an ancient bookcase, searched one of the crammed shelves for a minute, and pulled out an old hand-drawn map of Elyzandrium. He unfolded it and placed it on the dusty floor, then pointed to it with his stubby finger.

"The air-balloon station is here, and the main square is here." Alfred's finger came down and indicated the spots as he spoke. "Timmy, you saw the same thing here; and Simon, Jasper, and Casper, you noticed it around the baker's shop, here, and also around here. I saw it here and here."

He marked all the places with copper coins. They looked at the coins. They formed a shape almost like a circle.

"Now look. Do you see what I see?"

They all nodded. Flores's paw pointed to the area in the middle of the coins.

"Assuming that there is someone who is somehow

stealing these children's laughter, he would send his gangs out to collect the kids in all directions, wouldn't he?"

"Or she," Timmy interjected.

Flores ignored him and studied the map more closely. In the area in the middle of the coins were several large structures joined together. They were surrounded by a tall wall.

"What is this?" Flores asked.

Alfred leaned in to get a closer look.

"An old factory. It's been abandoned for years. The wall makes it impossible to see inside from the street. And one of the structures is very tall. A good hiding spot."

Timmy slowly stood up.

"I think it's time we took a closer look at that factory." He turned to Flores. "Flores, your flying machine could come in handy. It would give us a good view of the area. May we borrow it?"

To Timmy's surprise, he sounded calm and collected.

"You guys?" she scoffed. "Not in a million years. It's a highly advanced machine." Then she smiled and added: "But I can fly it for you."

Chapter 9

THERE WAS ROOM for only two passengers in the flying machine. Simon was prone to airsickness, and Jasper and Casper were both eager to go but finally agreed (this took a moment's awkward discussion) that they were a little too heavy. So in the end, the duty fell to Timmy, and this was of course what he had hoped for all along. He was to borrow Simon's magical goggles so he could get a peek inside the abandoned factory.

Alfred checked his wind charts. He gazed for a long while through a peculiar-looking spyglass aimed at the sky and finally declared that tonight would be perfect flying weather. The sky would be clear, with light winds from the southwest.

It was therefore a huge embarrassment for Alfred that as evening fell, large storm clouds rolled in from the north. They were an angry dark gray, almost black,

and with them came a heavy rain. Soon the sound of thunder echoed across the mountains, and lightning bolts flashed with icy blue electricity across the sky. Deafening cracks jarred the group to the bone as nature unleashed its awesome power. The driving rain fell sideways, and the wind tore at the window shutters, making them clap and bang against the outside walls.

"Well," Alfred said finally. "My predictions were wrong. I must have looked at some outdated charts, or perhaps the spyglass needs some adjusting."

Timmy suggested that they wait until the following night, but Flores wouldn't hear it. "I'm an excellent pilot. A little weather can't deter me." Timmy was about to object when one of the shutters blew open, and wind and rain hammered into the room. Alfred quickly hurried over and managed to close the window.

"See?" Flores declared. "We'll have a strong tailwind. Perfect!"

At that, Timmy gave up. They discussed the plan. Flores was to circle the factory compound at least twice, as close as she could get, while Timmy used the goggles to look inside. The goggles had been designed to work well at night, even if the image quality would be a little grainier. Should anything out of the ordinary happen, or if anyone spied them, they would dash out of there as quickly as possible. Simple.

It was a five-minute walk to where the flying machine was parked, but it took about three times as long to get there because they were walking against the rain and wind. It howled around them. Flores's voice was barely audible as she turned to Timmy:

"You okay? Try to keep up!"

Timmy had borrowed a spare helmet from Flores, and he was just in the process of trying it on when she turned around. It was way too big, and at that very moment it was down over his eyes, and he knew he must have looked like a fool. *Typical,* he thought. He was drenched through and feeling quite miserable.

They finally reached the airplane. It was parked under a shed, and for the first time Timmy got a proper look at it. It wasn't very big, but it had three rows of wings on the front and two at the back. The tail was split in two. A wooden frame held it all together, and cloth was stretched tightly over everything. There were wires and pulleys and cogs and exhaust pipes all over the body of it. It looked like a mess, Timmy thought, but Flores insisted that it was the best flying machine ever built.

"Who built it?" Timmy asked.

"I did, of course!" Flores answered.

They climbed on board. There were two seats, one behind the other, and Timmy sat in the back. He was secretly grateful for that, so that she wouldn't see how afraid he might get. He was actually quite scared of flying but had neglected to mention that to anyone. He had been too eager to impress Flores.

Before they took off, he asked (just in case anything unforeseen should happen) if there was any kind of device that might be used to jump from the plane with, like a big sheet that could strap to their backs and inflate to break their fall, or something like that. Flores didn't know about such a thing, and thought it was the most ridiculous idea she had ever heard. Instead she told him to strap in properly and pressed the starter button.

The steam-powered double propeller started with a loud bang. There was lots of black smoke, and then the wooden blades started whipping viciously through the air. Flores gave the plane some throttle, and the engine roared. They rolled out of the shed and swung left, past some trash cans, as the speed and noise increased. To Timmy's horror, they were now heading straight for a building. He tried to point this out by wildly waving his arms and screaming at the top of his lungs, but Flores couldn't hear a thing over the noise.

Instead she gave the plane even more throttle, and the machine jerked forward, bouncing and skidding over the cobblestones. He immediately regretted having been so keen to accompany Flores.

Rain whipped Timmy's face, and he had a hard time seeing anything at all, just glimpses and flashes. The tips of the wings must have been only inches from the walls on both sides, but that didn't seem to bother Flores either. The flying machine just barreled forward, and the building ahead grew bigger and bigger. Timmy was stiff with terror. They would surely crash into it in a few seconds, exploding like a fireball. Realizing that his life might be ending, Timmy supposed he was okay with that. He had lived a short but rich life. Good friends, grand adventures, and all that. But it had been a short life. He wished he could have lived just a few more years, maybe even had a chance to travel and see some of the world. Alas, it was not to be. He squeezed his eyes shut and waited for the inevitable.

When Timmy and Flores were what seemed like only a few feet from imminent death, the plane rose almost vertically, just barely missing the chimneys of the building.

Timmy could feel himself soar upward, pinned to the back of the seat. His stomach did somersaults, and his throat was sore from screaming. He looked down

and saw rooftops. They were just regular rooftops, but he thought they were the most beautiful rooftops he had ever seen, simply because he was still alive.

A second after they were airborne, the wind took them. It jerked them violently sideways, then up, then down again. The plane was like a rolled-up ball of paper in the massive force of the storm. He could see Flores struggling with the controls. The sharp bang of a lightning bolt tore through the air right next to them, and again he thought about his much-too-short life. Why had he volunteered for this? Who did he think he was, with this whole ninja crime-fighting business?

And he wouldn't even get to die fighting like a ninja. He would die from falling from the sky in a little machine of cloth, metal, and wood. All he could do was hang on for dear life.

But Flores hadn't exaggerated about her skill as a pilot. She countered every blow, somehow defying gravity and keeping them up in the air. The wind and rain still whipped them this way and that, but now they had gained some altitude, and Timmy felt the tight grip of fear on his heart loosen a little bit. He swallowed hard and looked out over the city.

It was actually a beautiful sight to see, and the

lightning and storm clouds made the view even more magnificent. The bamboo skyscrapers were lit from within and looked like strange shining beacons through the rain. When lightning flashed, it lit up the entire city like daylight. Then darkness would return and a million glittering lights would glow through the clouds from below.

Flores looked back and shouted something.

"Haven't you ever been in a tiny flying machine in a lightning storm before?"

"No!"

She laughed at this.

"Neither have I!"

This amused her to no end, and Timmy could hear her laughing wildly through the wind.

Timmy smiled. Flores was obviously a little crazy. He found that he liked that about her.

The good thing about flying in a lightning storm was that there were no other machines in the air that night. If anyone was in the factory, they would never suspect that anyone was spying on them from the air. Not on a night like this.

After a few minutes, Flores pointed to something below them: the abandoned factory. It was shrouded in rain, barely visible in the darkness, but it lit up sharply whenever a lightning bolt struck nearby, and then they could see it quite clearly.

The factory had many buildings, but one stood much taller than the rest. It looked more like an ancient abandoned castle than a factory, and its stone façades had intricate carvings, like those on an old cathedral. There were smokestacks and dozens of chimneys, and hundreds of dark windows that looked like black holes in the walls.

Flores swooped down. The erratic winds tossed them around, but she held on, and they soared in a wide angle around the complex.

"Get closer!" Timmy shouted.

He put on the goggles and scanned the buildings as the plane got within range. He had to fiddle a bit with them to adjust the distance, but after he got the hang of it, he was amazed at how effective they were. He could see inside rooms, even in almost total darkness. Magic goggles indeed.

At first, Timmy couldn't spot anything unusual. Just empty rooms with abandoned factory equipment sitting around. Hallways, big rooms, small rooms. No movement, no sound. He tapped Flores on the shoulder, indicating that she should bring the plane around again. She gave a thumbs-up and did as he'd asked.

This time he focused on the taller structures and adjusted the goggles so that he could see farther in. And there, a figure! It was standing perfectly still. On the top of its head, he could make out two odd shapes,

like tall ears. To Timmy, they looked like rabbit ears. He thought he saw more movement. Was someone else there too? Timmy tried to zoom in, but it was difficult with the plane bobbing up and down. Still, he got enough of a glimpse to know who the other figures

were. He recognized seven thick necks attached to seven stocky bodies. The Gribbles!

There was definitely something going on inside this supposedly abandoned factory.

Timmy tapped Flores on the shoulder again and gave her a thumbs-up. She increased the throttle and pointed the machine upward.

But just as they were about to fly off, Timmy saw the figure with the tall ears rush up to the window. It pointed straight at them.

"They saw us! Get us out of here!" he shouted.

Flores maxed the throttle, darting the plane away and up. They took cover in the dark clouds, and for a while all they could see was gray and black, and flashes of blinding white light as bolts of lightning shot past them with thunderous crackles.

Timmy decided to just squeeze his eyes shut and try to pass out.

Many violent jolts and jerks later, they were back on the ground. Timmy stumbled out of the plane, trying not to let his knees buckle.

Chapter 10

"HE SAW YOU? Are you sure? And he had long ears, like a rabbit?"

Alfred had listened intently to Timmy and Flores's report of the flight, and now he was leaning forward with a serious face.

"This is not good," he continued as they both nodded. He tugged slowly at his long, thin beard. "I knew this time would come."

It was the first time any of them had seen Alfred so anxious. Jasper and Casper made calculations on their notepads and squabbled silently about whether the level of concern was ten or ten point five on a scale of one to ten.

Timmy looked at Flores. She had softened toward him just a bit and had even given him half a smile while they'd walked back to the toy shop through the rain. It wasn't much, but it was a start. Now she sat looking serious, with a little frown.

"You know who this rabbit is?" she asked.

Alfred looked even more troubled. He shifted in his seat before he answered.

"I do." He paused a moment. "I made him."

The five friends looked at him with shared apprehension.

"You made him? So he's a toy?" Timmy asked with unease.

"You could say that. Not quite a toy, but something I made when I was much younger, and much more stupid. When I thought I could make anything." He looked at Timmy. "You remember the flower you picked for me in the caves? I told you I had last seen it forty years ago. It was with that flower that I built the

Blue Rabbit. Created, you could say. But I was young, and I didn't know what I was doing. I had underestimated the power of that flower, and my creation came out terribly wrong."

"Why did you make it?" Casper asked.

"Because," Alfred blurted out, "the king at that time commissioned it from me. The Blue Rabbit was meant to be a toy for his daughter's birthday. Right away I realized that something had gone wrong, that the toy had gained too much power. It grew large and it grew intelligent. It started to turn into something out of my control. It broke my other toys out of jealousy. When I tried to stop it . . . well, I couldn't. He used my own magic on me. He must have seen me mix the ingredients. I was paralyzed."

He paused. Timmy could tell Alfred had kept all this inside for a very long time. Alfred finally took a breath and continued.

"So as you can imagine, I could never give the king's daughter this toy. I finally managed to take control of the situation again, but before I could destroy it—or *him,* rather—he escaped."

"What happened to him?" Flores asked.

"I don't know exactly. Last time I saw Rabbit, he had stolen a steam balloon and was sailing away across the mountains. Later, I heard he had made a home somewhere in a foreign land."

"And now he's back," Simon said.

"And now he's back...." The toymaker's voice sounded sad.

"To steal children's laughter." Timmy looked glum. "What does he want with children's laughter?"

"I'm not sure. I've never heard of such a thing before. But as good as magic can be, it can also be turned into bad. Dark magic. He's up to something."

"Well, we'll stop him!" Flores exclaimed.

At first, the room was quiet. Timmy's gaze wandered from each of his friends to the next. It finally landed back on Alfred. Timmy gathered his courage and stood up.

"Yes." He straightened. "There's nothing we can't

do. If the Blue Rabbit is as bad as you say he is, we'll find a way to stop him. Whatever he's up to. We are ninja crime fighters, after all."

Alfred nodded. One after another, the others nodded too. Best of all, Timmy noticed that Flores was smiling at him.

"Okay." He looked around at his friends once again. "Only we know what's going on. Only we have the ability, the responsibility, to stop him. If we don't, an entire generation of kids might lose their ability to laugh, and we don't know who his next victim will be. I, for one, do not want to wait around and find out."

He sat down again. He hated to have to make those little speeches. He worried that it didn't suit him, or that he sounded bossy, even though he was pretty sure he knew what he was talking about. If he'd had a choice of what to do with an evening like this, he would have liked to take Flores to a movie, and be really funny, and make her realize who he was, that he was a cool cat, then take her for a romantic walk in the park, and maybe even go on another crazy ride in her flying machine. This time in good weather. That was what he wanted. Not to give inspirational speeches about doing the right thing.

Some distance away, in the abandoned factory, the Blue Rabbit stood alone on a balcony, eating a pastry.

He loved pastries more than anything. Right now, he was having a chocolate éclair and loving every second of it. Behind him, on a table, was a small mountain of chocolate éclairs. By the end of the evening, he would have consumed at least fourteen of them.

He turned and looked around at the empty room. It pleased him that it was empty. He always felt cranky after seeing the Gribble cousins. Once, they had been useful. They had collected parts for his machine, and they had brought him children whose laughter would power it. It hadn't been very difficult for them to find these kids. Children were everywhere. It was like picking flowers, the Blue Rabbit mused. Little innocent flowers. All the Gribble cousins had to do was collect them and bring them here. How hard could that have possibly been? He had even let them become captains and had given them the responsibility of recruiting other gangs so he could collect more laughter.

The Gribble captains. What a laugh. What a disaster. He had been good to the Gribbles. Had made them rich. Once, he had even let them smell one of his éclairs.

And now, in return, they had let him down. They had come to him with a children's tale. A tale about a gang of "ninjas" that had hindered their work and then given them a good beating. Bah! Couldn't they at least have been a little more creative when making up their story? Ninjas? Really? The Rabbit didn't mind the beating— the Gribbles deserved as much—but he minded that the Gribbles hadn't done their duty. He had really needed a boy puppy for one of his ingredients.

He knew plenty of other gang members he could make into captains, and who he would let smell the éclairs. He couldn't tolerate incompetence or insubordination. He had therefore decided that it was time for the Gribbles to end their employment with him. Unfortunately for the Gribbles, that meant death. Oh, they should have seen this coming; they should have known there was small print in the contract. Who doesn't read the contract? And, well, of course they had been upset. But what else could he do? If word spread that the Blue Rabbit was soft on his employees, then what would happen? Then everyone would expect him to be soft, wouldn't they? It would be absolute chaos. Mutiny. Anarchy. No, it would be no good. No good at all.

He took another bite of the chocolate éclair and mused as he chewed. It would be swift; he had seen to that. He wasn't really worried about the Gribbles. That problem would take care of itself. What worried him, what genuinely vexed him, was this affair with the flying machine. He had seen it fly in, of course, but then it had kept on flying around his compound. *His* compound. Sneaking, peeking, snooping around. He hadn't liked it. Not one bit.

But he had gotten a good look at them. Through his eyepiece, he had seen both of them. Oh yes. Two cats— kittens, really. Yes, he had seen them. Brave, though, venturing out in that weather. But why snoop around? In the middle of a storm? Oh, how brash. Thought maybe they would be hidden from his view? Maybe. Perhaps. Two very misguided cats. He hadn't imagined them. He had seen them, hadn't he? Yes, he had.

And the flying machine would be easy to find again. He had his connections. This was a one-off, a unique design, so it wouldn't be difficult to locate. It was a girl cat pilot, if he hadn't been mistaken. In fact, he could probably use her for something. Yes, he probably could. She had skills. There was real talent there, maneuvering that craft through the storm, he had seen that. So maybe even . . . maybe she could be the one to provide him with that other thing he had heard about. What did they call it? The thing that seemed to

be so important to the living? Love. Yes, that was it. He would need it, after he was reborn, as he liked to think of it. To be alive meant you had to love, apparently, and he wanted the full experience. Yes, with her skills, she might make a good fit. It was soon now. The machine was almost finished, and he would finally gain the only thing he didn't have.

He would find her. Yes, he would. His captains would. Gack and the Iguana boys. And bring her here.

Wouldn't be hard to find a girl cat pilot. Not at all. And the other one? The one with the curious goggles, peering in at him? Well, if Rabbit could find one, he could find the other, couldn't he? Yes, he could. After all, curiosity killed the cat, didn't it? Yes, it did. It would just be a matter of time.

He took the last bite of the éclair and got cream all over his blue fur. He walked over to the table, picked up a napkin, and wiped his fur very, very carefully. Then he helped himself to another éclair.

Chapter 11

THE MORNING WAS crisp and bright. It was as if the storm had wiped the sky clean, and now there was just clear blue. Timmy woke and wiped the sleep from his eyes. He got up on an elbow, yawned, and let his legs drop to the floor. They hung there while he slowly let them wake up and regain some sense of feeling. He had slept uncomfortably, waking up often and half gazing around the room.

When he had finally fallen back asleep, he'd had nightmares. The Blue Rabbit had been in them, but Timmy had only ever been able to glimpse him or see his shadow. The Rabbit's fur had been wet and had smelled funny, like something he had smelled before but couldn't place. Although now the dreams were fading into obscurity, as they always seemed to do.

Timmy yawned again and spread his toes out. It made him wake up a little more when he spread his toes.

Alfred was already up; Timmy could smell the coffee

in the air. Timmy didn't care for coffee himself, but he drank the milk that Alfred put into a little pitcher next to his coffee. Alfred always had a cup in the morning. It was the only time he drank anything besides tea.

Timmy walked into the little kitchen area.

"Hey, Alfred."

"Hi, Timmy."

Alfred's voice seemed low and without its usual spark.

"What's the matter?" Timmy hopped up onto the

chair opposite. Alfred sat grasping his mug of coffee. Then he let his eyes look into Timmy's. At first Alfred wasn't going to let on how he felt, but looking at the little gray cat in front of him, he felt a curious sense of companionship.

"I just don't know what I've dragged you into . . . ," Alfred began slowly.

"You haven't dragged us into anything," Timmy replied. "This is just happening. It was our own idea to become a ninja gang. It sounds really silly to say it now, but I did this because I felt I was finally doing something important. I was just a street cat once. I failed at school, didn't fit in. It bored me. I always thought

there was more to life than falling in line with everyone else. And now, it finally feels like I'm making a difference."

Alfred peered at Timmy inquiringly.

"I just feel responsible," Alfred began. "I made Rabbit all those years ago and know how powerful he became. And I encouraged you to become a ninja gang. And now you're face to face with him."

"You didn't know it was the Blue Rabbit at the time."

"No, I suppose I didn't. I just worry, that's all."

"Don't worry, Alfred. We'll manage okay."

"I know, Timmy. You are the bravest creature I have ever met."

For the second time in just a few days, Timmy blushed under his fur. Alfred smiled glumly and looked out the window. The sun was streaming in, and all was very peaceful.

The calm before the storm, Timmy thought.

Flores's voice from the doorway startled them both.

"Hey, boys." She leaned casually against the doorframe. "I'm gonna go see to the plane. Check on any damages from last night."

Timmy looked at her. She looked radiant in the morning light. No bags under her eyes from bad dreams, like he had. Didn't she ever worry about anything?

"Just make sure you're back before dark. We plan

everything tonight. We need your skill as a pilot to pull this off," Alfred said.

"Oh, I'll be back before a rhinoceros can say 'pot-belly,'" she answered with a snicker.

With that peculiar statement, she was off. Timmy went up to the window and watched her stride down the street. Alfred smiled behind him.

"You like her."

Timmy took a moment to answer.

"Yes, maybe a little."

"Go ahead. Go help her look over the flying machine."

"She'll be fine."

"I'm sure she could use some company."

Timmy was out the door. Flores was way ahead of him, so he upped his pace. He called out to her, but she didn't hear him. He jogged a little farther and called out again. She turned and saw him.

"What?" she yelled back.

A buzzing sound that had been in the background grew in strength. Timmy couldn't quite place it. He slowed to a walk.

"I just wanted to . . ." And then he saw where the noise was coming from.

A dozen or so steam-powered motorcycles were coming up the street toward Flores. They were coming

fast, too fast for comfort. He turned and saw more of them behind him. As they passed, he saw that all the drivers had scales, like reptiles. They wore big iron helmets and had leather jackets with studs in them.

On the sides of their bikes, they carried nets. This was not good.

"Flores! Watch out!" he yelled.

But as he watched, the first motorcycles reached

her. They circled her, kicking up dirt and dust. The noise from their engines was loud and sharp. He saw the riders heckling her, laughing as they went round and round, trapping her. She tried to run, but the circle of motorcycles was blocking her. Then the riders threw their nets. Flores skillfully avoided the first ones. Timmy began running toward her, his heart beating wildly.

He ran for all he was worth, faster than he ever had before, but he realized he would never make it. He was just too far away. As he watched in horror, they overcame her, and she was knocked down and trapped in the nets. Then there was another loud noise, coming from the sky. Timmy looked up and saw an air balloon swooping down fast, with steam pipes on its sides spewing smoke. In the carriage underneath stood a furry blue creature with long ears: the Blue Rabbit.

As Timmy watched in shock, Flores was lifted up into the air balloon, struggling against the nets. The Blue Rabbit grabbed her and hoisted her on board, and the balloon quickly ascended amid plumes of smoke.

"No!" Timmy shouted as he ran.

But when he finally reached the spot, the balloon was already high up in the air, and the bikes had sped off. Gasping for breath, he stopped and looked up.

The balloon was now just a speck in the blue sky, moving swiftly across the city. Timmy felt sick and angry. It felt like a kick to the gut. A minute ago, he had felt invincible, like nothing could stop him. Now, without Flores, he felt hopelessness seize his heart.

Chapter 12

THE AIR WAS heavy with gloom that evening in the toy shop. Timmy sat with his head in his paws, staring at the floor. He couldn't believe this had happened. He had dragged Flores into this. Because he fancied her. Now she was in the clutches of a villain who would steal that vibrant laughter from her. Timmy felt utterly defeated.

For a moment, he wished he could just return to the baker's loft and stay there. Stay out of trouble. Invent things. Continue with his life.

Except he couldn't.

He heard footsteps and looked up. Alfred was standing over him, holding a little wooden box. The man slowly sat down next to Timmy.

They sat in silence for a while, Alfred still clutching the box and Timmy with his head in his paws. Another few minutes ticked by. Timmy glanced at the box. He finally spoke with a small voice.

"What's in the box?"

Alfred peered down at him, a slow smile forming.

"Why, it's something for you."

He opened the box. Timmy looked over. He had to scoot closer to see.

It was the blue flower he had picked and spent at least two of his lives on. It lay there at the bottom of the box, looking like any other flower. Maybe just smaller and a little shriveled.

"Doesn't look like much."

"It doesn't, does it? But I'll tell you something. It has dried a few days now and has reached a perfect stage of dryness. It is in its most powerful state," Alfred said solemnly.

"Is that right?"

"That's right. I was thinking maybe I could make you something with it. What do you think? You picked it, after all."

Alfred paused, waiting for a reaction. Timmy looked at the flower. It didn't look magical at all.

"But maybe there is no point. . . ." Alfred's voice sank as he continued. "Maybe you have given up. And anyone would understand if you had. You have that look, like there is no point in going on. So maybe I will save it for later. For someone else."

"Yeah."

"Yes. . . . Might be best."

Alfred nodded slowly, looking out over the room as he continued in a low voice, almost to himself:

"It would be a very powerful magical device that I could create with this flower . . . but I suppose I could give it to another ninja cat when he comes along."

Timmy slowly raised his head. He glanced sideways at Alfred.

"How powerful?"

"Pretty powerful." Alfred sounded somber.

"Well . . . maybe there is still a point. In going on, I mean. A small point. Tiny point," Timmy finally said.

"You think so?" Alfred looked at him, his eyebrows raised.

"Yes, maybe."

"Maybe?"

"Well, what I mean is that . . . it's important to me to make sure Flores is okay."

"In that case, maybe I should make you something after all. But you would have to promise to use it properly. And do it soon, because time is running out."

"I thought maybe it was already too late. For Flores, I mean."

"No, there's still time. If there's anything I know in this world, it's magic. Collecting laughter takes preparation and time."

"So you think Flores might still be okay?"

"I do. But not for much longer. You would have to hurry."

"I could do that," Timmy said in a small voice.

"So yes?" Alfred raised his eyebrows again, a soft smile spreading on his lips.

"Yes."

"Okay, then. Good. I will set to work immediately."

"What will you make?"

"I don't know yet. The flower will tell me. It will show itself."

"Okay."

"And in the meantime, try to cheer up. Despite what has happened, the game isn't lost yet. We have lots of work to do. Lots of preparations to make."

Alfred got up. He closed the box and disappeared into his lab.

Timmy was left sitting alone again. But now he could feel his willpower seep back into his heart. He was going to do this. He would defeat this wretched Blue Rabbit. He straightened his spine and walked tall into the shop room.

It wasn't hard for Timmy to convince the gang to join him in this final quest. "We all like Flores," Jasper said.

"Even if she's been a bit hard on us at times," Casper added. "And it isn't only about her anyway. It's about all those kids."

"One thing, though, guys," said Simon. "We need to come up with a good name for ourselves. Not 'Ninja Timmy and His Gang.'"

They agreed they would all put their minds to it.

That afternoon, the most unusual thing happened. They were all sitting together, planning the rescue operation, realizing what a gigantic task it would be for only four friends, when there was a knock on the door. Alfred had closed the shop for the day in order to work in peace, and there was a big sign on the door saying Closed.

"Who could it be?" murmured Jasper.

Casper went to the door. "We're not open today! Who's there?"

There was only a muffled, inaudible reply. Casper turned to the others, trying to decide if he should open the door. Another loud knock rattled the door. Casper did a quick calculation in his head. A burglar wouldn't knock; he would simply break in. If whoever was out there had seen the sign and understood it, they had to be a friend of Alfred's. If they didn't understand the sign, they were probably from out of town and perhaps in need of assistance. And what kind of crime-fighting gang would these four friends be if they didn't lend a hand to those in need? He made a mental list of all the foreign languages in which he knew the phrase "Good afternoon" and opened the door.

Casper's jaw dropped. He hadn't been so surprised and frightened at the same time since he was just a little kid, and Jasper, dressed up as a pirate, had jumped out of a closet in the middle of the night.

In front of him stood Dobie Gribble, the biggest of the Gribble cousins. He smiled meekly at Casper. In his hand was a box of chocolates, which he held up. The piglet and the wild boar stood like that for what seemed like several minutes—Casper in shock with his mouth open, and Dobie with a silly smile, waiting for Casper to take the chocolates. Across the street stood

the rest of the Gribbles, waiting anxiously to see what was going to happen.

"Friends?" Dobie finally said.

"Good afternoon?" was all Casper could come up with to say.

"Friends?" Dobie repeated. "Let bygones be bygones? Water under the bridge and all that?"

At this point, Timmy and the others had all come up to the door. They gathered behind Casper, staring at the tense scene in amazement.

"You see," Dobie continued, "we know that our two gangs started off, shall we say, on a bad foot. And there were some misunderstandings, and differences of opinion, and some scuffles, and a lot of running."

"That must be the greatest understatement of all time, but sure, yes. And what do you want? What's with the box of chocolates?" Timmy said, who had now come up to stand next to Casper.

"Well, see, we all discussed it, and that seems to be the thing to give someone when, well, you want to say . . . ehm, sorry."

"You've come here to apologize for being the most despicable gang of boars to ever wander the streets of Elyzandrium?"

"That pretty much sums it up, yes."

"And why would you want to do that?" Timmy was both highly suspicious and genuinely interested.

"We would like to be friends." Dobie turned to his cousins for encouragement. "Yes, friends, that's it," Dobie said as the rest of the Gribbles behind him nodded in unison. Timmy wasn't having it. He thought for sure this was some kind of foul trick, or a strange form of ambush.

"Well, we're not sure we want to be friends with you guys."

Dobie was beginning to look desperate and again held forward the chocolates. He was looking around nervously now, as if there were something about to spring from around the corner and hurt him.

"No? But we brought chocolates, see?" He held the box up higher.

"We're not falling for one of your tricks!" Timmy's tone was sharp. His tail wagged back and forth in irritation. Dobie looked frustrated.

"But you must help us! We need your protection! The Rabbit is going to kill us!"

"What? Kill you? I thought you worked for him!"

"Not anymore. Not since you guys whooped our behinds! Apparently there's some really tiny print in our employment contract that clearly specifies death if we fail to finish a job! When we returned without the puppy that night, the night when you whooped our behinds, he was terribly upset, you see. Then he showed us the contract . . . and now he's after us and is going to kill us."

The last sentence was nothing more than a whisper.

Dobie sounded legitimately scared. He looked nervous and miserable, and Timmy thought he even spotted a tear forming in the corner of his eye.

"Oh, please . . . please, please, please, please!" He was begging now. "I'm too young to die. . . ." And now the tear dropped onto the stone step where he was standing.

Timmy exhaled and looked at the others. They seemed equally at a loss. Simon shrugged. Casper and Jasper stood with their notepads out, scribbling furiously, but they couldn't come up with an equation that made any sense. Alfred shrugged too, then nodded. Timmy turned back to Dobie, still suspicious.

"Well, come in, then. But if you try anything, we'll whoop your behinds again, and this time so you won't be able to sit for weeks! And don't touch anything!"

With that, he stepped aside, and Dobie and the other Gribble cousins hurried inside.

A few minutes later, they all sat in one of the back rooms, eating chocolates. Alfred took a break from his work to taste some. Timmy and the others were still wary but were going to let the Gribbles explain their case.

Dobie began by introducing all his cousins: Sly, Wheezer, Tribble, Dibble, and Fibbledee and Fibbledoo (they were the youngest). Seven in all. The ninja friends pretty much forgot who was who right away.

Dobie started to explain how they had come to work for the Blue Rabbit some months back. "See, at first he was really nice, complimenting us on our large stature and our impressive thick necks. We ran some errands for him and helped move oversize materials, that sort of business. There was apparently a machine he was building that required a lot of heavy lifting. Oh, and he paid us well. But then the threats began. Rabbit had made us steal stuff, and if we didn't, he threatened to hurt us in unspeakable ways. I can't remember exactly how he was going to hurt us, just that there were lightning bolts coming from his eyes when he spoke. That was when he ordered us to bring him children, and we

never dared ask why. Luckily, the kids were okay when he was done with them. After a few days, he had me and the others return the kids to where we'd found them. From then on, it was a downward spiral. Our missions became more frequent, and we stole, or 'borrowed,' as Rabbit calls it, more and more kids. Rabbit threatened that if we stopped, he would turn us over to the city guard. By now, with the Iguanas, his machine must be almost complete."

Timmy and the others listened attentively. The story seemed clear enough, even believable. If the machine was close to being operational, there was no time to lose.

And the Gribbles did come across as quite regretful for their bad behavior and kept apologizing. "It was because we're big boys," they would say. They explained how they were always teased in school for being big and how everyone assumed they were dumb jocks.

"But we're not that dumb!" piped up Wheezer. Someone had hired them, and it had made them feel important. Like they had found their place in life. Well, at least before the threats had begun.

Dobie finally stopped and looked at the four friends and Alfred pleadingly.

"Could we stay here awhile? Perhaps we could even be of some help? Is there any heavy lifting to be done?"

The friends shared a serious look. Timmy turned back to Dobie.

"Wait here," he said sternly.

The friends gathered in another room to discuss matters. Everyone agreed that the Gribbles seemed sincere and that the chocolates had been delicious. They even felt sorry for the Gribbles. But it also seemed quite unnatural to simply forgive and forget. Casper suggested that as a condition of accepting the Gribbles' apology, they should make them bring chocolates every day. Jasper did a quick calculation and suggested that twice a day would be more appropriate. They all thought Jasper's math made a lot of sense. Perhaps they would also make them lift some seriously heavy things.

At the end of the day, said Timmy, he supposed it would be a sign of greatness to forgive these culprits. That was what great figures in history had done. It would be noble. And being noble would be right in line with how they wanted their crime-fighting ninja gang to be perceived.

"Furthermore," Simon added, "the Gribbles might come in very handy when the plan to find Flores is put into action. They'd add some much-needed muscle to the gang." Everyone nodded at this.

So it was decided that they would let the Gribbles stay. The cousins wouldn't be full members of the group—at least, not yet. They would have to prove themselves first. If they did well in the next day's rescue operation, lifted lots of heavy stuff, and weren't late with the chocolates, then maybe they could even begin as trainees.

The group spent the rest of the afternoon coming up with a plan of attack. The Gribbles turned out to be pretty helpful. They knew the layout of the factory and where Rabbit might be keeping Flores and the children. Apparently, after the laughter-extraction procedure was over, the children would be put into dark and scary rooms, to give them a taste of what it would be like to never laugh again.

"The extraction happens in Rabbit's lab," Dobie said. "The laughter is collected in glass jars that are then sealed."

"That's how my grandma makes strawberry jam," said Jasper.

"It was peach jam, if you recall," Casper countered.

"Focus!" cried Simon.

The brothers quieted down and let Dobie continue:

"The jars are transported to a room on the top floor, and Rabbit wheels them away in a red wagon. The laughter would work like fuel for the machine. Word on the street is that with the help of the Iguana gang, the Rabbit has almost completed it."

"Oh, I know the Iguanas." Alfred shivered. "They're bad news."

"Apparently, the leader of the Iguana gang, Gack, and the Rabbit are bonding over their love of éclairs," Dobie added. "Anyway, the best way to get in is through the balconies on the upper levels. That way we can sneak by the Iguanas, who are probably patrolling the gate around the compound. That means we'll have to fly there to avoid them."

"But how will we fly without Flores here to pilot?" asked Jasper.

Just then, Timmy realized that all his friends were looking at him expectantly.

"No. Not a chance. No way." Timmy actually physically took a step back. "I almost died in that thing." But even as he spoke, he knew all his reasons why and realized that colorful retellings of his near-death experience would fall on deaf ears.

After much persuasion from the others, Timmy agreed that he maybe, possibly, perhaps with a lot of luck, could manage to fly it. And most likely crash it.

"I'm good pals with the old captain who runs the air-balloon station"—they had lifted a lot of heavy equipment for him—"and we might be able to borrow one of the balloons," said Dobie. "We could fly right next to you."

The discussion and planning continued until late.

On a crude map of the abandoned factory, they marked strategically important points and possible escape routes. The basic plan was that the Gribbles would deal with the Iguanas, and Timmy and his gang would find and rescue the kids and Flores.

Nobody mentioned what would happen when they came face to face with the Rabbit himself, since nobody really had a good plan for that. It worried Timmy, but there were so many other obstacles facing them that he figured they would simply cross that bridge when they came to it.

After they had gone through every detail for the third time, they finally fell silent. It seemed they were really going to attempt this. Timmy felt scared, but he could also feel a strange calm. He knew they were doing the right thing by saving Flores and the children. They would try their best but would also let Fate play her role. He latched on to that feeling and tried not to think of anything at all. It would go as it would go.

It was at that moment that Alfred stepped into the room. He looked at Timmy.

"It is ready," Alfred said.

Chapter 13

FLORES OPENED HER eyes. Her muscles ached, and when she tried to move, she realized in horror that she was still bound. She strained against the thick ropes, but they didn't budge. The room was dark and cold. High above, she could make out giant crystal chandeliers hanging from the ceiling.

Anger pulsed through her. It hadn't been fair; there had been too many Iguanas. She hated unfair fights. Those hideous, spiteful lizards on their noisy bikes! And they stank. And their little motorcycles stank too.

She remembered hearing Timmy calling out to her, and spinning and being really happy to see him. Happy that he had come to see her off. She was really beginning to like that Timmy. But her joy had turned to anger at that awful racket the bikes had made, and at the dust and dirt being kicked up into her face. Then the nets had come flying.

It was an awful feeling to be trapped, unable to fight back. It was also a new feeling, as Flores had never been powerless in her life. But what could she have done when she'd been hoisted into the air, face to face with a furry blue rabbit peering at her with his red eyes? Then her vision had gone black.

"When I get into the same room with that blue rabbit again," she murmured, "I will show him who he is dealing with."

"Hello. Are you awake now?" a voice said.

The Blue Rabbit stepped toward her. She wondered if he had been standing in the shadows all along.

He was tall for a rabbit. Probably six feet tall. He wore a long black coat draped over his brilliantly blue fur. He was chewing on something that looked to Flores like an éclair.

"How do you feel? I hope my boys didn't hurt you," he continued.

Flores struggled against the ropes, but it was hopeless. She shifted and managed to sit up against the wall behind her.

"Release me!" she roared.

Blue Rabbit peered at her blankly with his little red eyes, wiping his mouth carefully with a napkin.

"But I just captured you. That wouldn't make much sense, now, would it?"

"You . . . you crook! You no-good, long-eared, furry

freak! You don't know who you're dealing with! Untie
these ropes, or I will . . . make you wish you'd never
been born!"

"Again, you make no sense at all. After all, I *was*
never born, per se."

Rabbit turned and walked across the room to a table, where he picked up another éclair. He took a bite and smacked his lips. The sweet smell of the pastry wafted up into his nostrils. His favorite smell. He had a thought, perhaps something that would calm the angry feline.

"Do you want to smell an éclair?" he asked.

"What? *Smell* an éclair? No!"

This rabbit character was clearly crazy. Smell an éclair?

"No? I was just being generous. Fine, no smelling for you."

Rabbit carefully stepped closer, moving in and out of the shadows, until he was standing right next to her. Flores looked up at him.

"My friends will come for me. You wait and see. Then you'll be sorry."

"Your friends? Oh good. Is that old grump Alfred with them? I would very much like to see old Alfred again. It's been so long since I've seen my creator."

Flores felt a shiver go up her spine. She tried to calm down. *Stay cool,* she thought. The night sky visible through the windows was a deep ultramarine, and she let her gaze fall on that.

"What do you want with me?" she asked slowly.

"I'm very sorry, but you may not ask questions. I will ask some of *you,* though, and I hope you can answer them. For your own sake."

"And if I don't?"

Rabbit just took another bite of the éclair and chewed. He looked at her calmly.

"Why were you spying on me? From that flying machine of yours?"

Flores just stared at the night sky.

"Were you looking for the children? Are they friends of yours? They are quite fine, save for one little detail, of course. You may think I am cruel to take away their laughter. But they can go on with their little lives quite well without it." Rabbit walked around, glancing at Flores to make sure she was listening. He continued.

"Lives, yes. Life . . . You see, those children can give

me the one thing I don't have. And I want it. The thing all of you take for granted. Only I seem to understand the true value of it." Rabbit paused, then spoke coldly and clearly. "Life, my dear feline friend. What you would call . . . a soul."

Flores stared at him. She suddenly felt sad for this creature. What a horrific way to go about getting a soul.

"So you're stealing the souls of innocent children in order to get one yourself?" she spat out, staring at him.

The Blue Rabbit made no sign of even hearing her. Instead he leaned down so his face was right next to hers. His voice was very soft.

"Who is that cat friend of yours? Why was he dressed like a ninja? Is he a real ninja or a fake who just dresses like one? Is he your, what do you call it . . . boyfriend? I would very much like to meet him too."

Flores pursed her lips. She wasn't going to say a thing.

"No? No answers?" Rabbit patted his delicate little mouth again with a napkin. Then his voice turned icy cold.

"Then you are of no use to me."

Rabbit lifted Flores by her nape (she hated that more than anything) and walked across the room. She dangled helplessly in his grasp. Through the windows, she could see the lights of the city far, far below.

In the floor by the windows was a trapdoor. Rabbit opened it. He held Flores over it and then dropped her into the black hole. And down she fell.

Chapter 14

ALFRED LED TIMMY and the gang into his workroom. Timmy could feel his heart race in anticipation. This was it. The concoction Alfred had created with the blue flower stood ready. Timmy knew this moment was as important to Alfred as it was to him. The old man's chance to right forty years of wrong. It was both frightening and exciting that Alfred was entrusting *him,* Timmy, with his device. It seemed that Alfred saw something in him that Timmy did not see himself. All Timmy knew was that he couldn't let Alfred down.

Alfred stopped and turned. He folded his hands behind his back, looked Timmy in the eye, and nodded once. Next to him, in the center of the room, was something covered with a large blanket. Timmy walked closer and stopped. He could feel the others pushing into his back, whispering excitedly. They all squeezed into the cramped workshop, trying to find somewhere

to stand, while trying their best not to knock down any of the books or tiny glass bottles that lined the shelves. A hush spread through the room. Everyone stood wide-eyed in anticipation. Alfred smiled at his captive audience.

"As you know, I didn't have much time." He paused for effect as he slowly moved behind the cloth. "And I didn't want to repeat the mistakes of the past. Harnessing the power of the blue flower known as *Eufsporia galitinos marillimus* was not easy. But I suppose I have learned a thing or two over the years. Only time will tell. The object that I have made does not look like much, but I hope it will do the trick."

He pulled the blanket away.

On a small table in front of Timmy stood a small bluish metal object. It didn't look like anything Timmy had ever seen before. It was more or less round, with something that looked like a dial on one side, and with a button made of brilliant blue stone on the top. The stone sparkled in the soft light.

The whispering behind Timmy started up again. He stepped up to the strange device, took it, and held it carefully in his paw. It was surprisingly heavy. Its smooth surface was cool to the touch, but as Timmy held it, he could feel a strange warmth surge through him. A tingling sensation came with it, spreading from his heart and sweeping through his body, all the way out to the tip of each strand of fur. It felt almost like a tickle that coursed through him, touching every nerve on its way. The sound around him faded, as if receding into a dream, and for that moment, the only sensation he had was that of the weight of the object in his paw. It seemed to grow even heavier and appeared to glow softly as he regarded it. Wisps of light curled up from it like smoke, then disappeared into thin air. Timmy felt completely aware, yet the room around him seemed distant.

The sensation lasted for only a moment. Then the glow faded, and the whispers of his friends filtered back into his consciousness. As he looked up, he could see how Alfred watched him intently, then smiled with recognition. He spoke calmly:

"What you are feeling is only a tickle of the power contained within. It is feeling you, as you are feeling it. In a way, it is alive—just like you. Powerful magic works that way. You could say that it is saying 'Hello, and nice to meet you.'"

Timmy shuddered involuntarily as the object's power receded into its cool blue shell. He put it back on the table.

"It feels very good," he finally said with a smile. "Strange, and a little scary, but good. And it looks quite nice."

"It's called a Ziliosphere," Alfred said.

"Ziliosphere," Timmy repeated softly.

He turned and saw how the others watched him in awe. Jasper and Casper had their notepads out but hadn't written a thing. Simon stood looking transfixed,

his fur for once ruffled. Dobie and the cousins just looked slack-jawed, much like they always did. Everyone stood spellbound, waiting for what would happen next. Alfred stepped forward, laid his hand on Timmy's shoulder, and said:

"Now, let me show you how this works."

Chapter 15

THE TROOP SILENTLY snuck through the alleys of Elyzandrium. A quarter moon hung like a giant slice of peach in the deep blue sky, reflecting on the slick cobblestones. They were all wearing varying degrees of ninja clothing—all black, of course—to blend in with the night. Some of them still even had the headbands.

As Timmy looked around at the ragtag gang, he felt a real sense of purpose. Nobody spoke. They would communicate with hand signals. After a moment, Timmy raised his paw and twisted his fingers into a signal, and he and Simon broke away. Nervously they headed down the alley where Flores's plane was parked.

They had arranged to rendezvous in the sky over the main square, Timmy and Simon in the flying machine and the others in the balloon they would borrow from Dobie's captain friend.

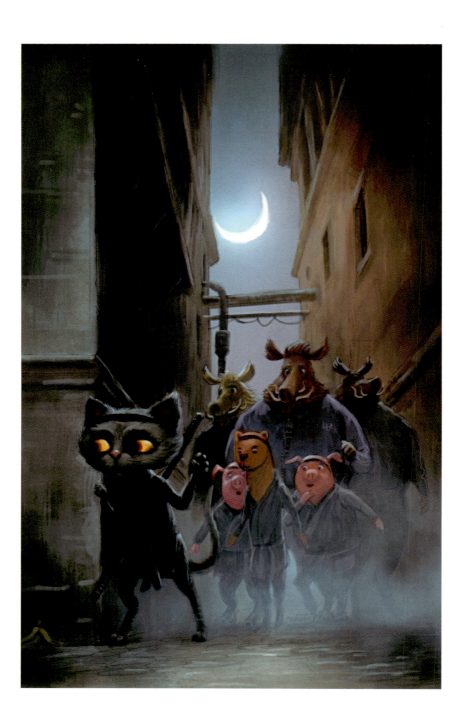

Getting the flying machine started was no joke. Maneuvering it on the ground was even harder, and Timmy feared how the taking-off-and-flying part was going to go. He didn't even want to think about the landing.

"So far, so good!" he cried over the whir of the engine as the plane rose. A few bricks from a chimney got knocked down, but he managed to get the thing off the ground, and they were airborne. As the cold night air rushed around him, he breathed a sigh of relief. He made a mental note to pay the people in that building a visit when all this was over and offer to repair what he had damaged.

Luckily there was no lightning storm to deal with, and soon they were circling over the main square, waiting for the air balloon to sail up.

The sky was clear as they soared over the city. The moon lit up a few billowy clouds, and a hundred thousand stars twinkled brilliantly above. Below them sprawled the vast city, sparkling with warm, familiar light. Timmy looked down and thought it looked beautiful, and felt lucky to live there. He dug his paw into his innermost pocket and felt the smooth, cold surface of the Ziliosphere Alfred had made for him. It comforted him. Somehow, at this moment, sitting high above the earth in a tiny machine made from wood, cloth, and steel, and held together with string, this small object gave him strength. He didn't know how things were going to turn out, but that was okay.

They now saw the hot-air balloon emerging through the clouds, streaming toward them. It was enormous.

It had three decks, hanging below several heavily ornamented balloons that had been strapped together with chain and rope. Multicolored flags and banners fluttered at the top. It actually looked more like a floating ship than an air balloon.

On the foredeck they saw Casper, Jasper, and the Gribbles. There was also a very old man among them, with an impressive white beard and a tall hat covered with medallions. Undoubtedly the captain. Timmy waved, and they waved back.

The balloon-ship was a bit slower than they were, so Timmy had to keep circling it while it slowly floated toward the old factory.

They reached it about twenty minutes later. It looked dark and abandoned, but by now they all knew better. Timmy suddenly remembered that he hadn't thought of where to land. There wasn't exactly a plane runway among the old structures.

There was only one option: to glide the plane onto the rickety roofs. The balloon-ship could pretty much tie on to anything, so he wasn't worried about them.

He looked back at Simon and gave a thumbs-up. He wasn't sure why he did that, but it seemed like an appropriate thing to do before landing on rooftops. Simon smiled back uncertainly and returned the gesture.

Timmy made a wide turn and lined up the flying machine. Then he pointed its nose down at the factory. The steep dive gave the plane unwanted speed,

and Timmy realized they were coming in too hot. No matter. Too late now.

He yanked at the controls. The wheels made contact with the first roof and immediately bounced off again. He jerked the controls forward, and the plane dipped down again at the very end of the roof. It hit hard and rebounded wildly up. Then there was a brief touchdown, almost sideways, on a tiny slanted piece of roof on the next structure, before the plane dropped again. It slammed down hard on a shingled roof on the following building. The wheels caught on a shingle and were ripped clean off. For a moment the craft floated, shingles flying in all directions, before it slammed violently into the next roof, caught on the edge, and stopped. They had landed.

However, the small piece of roof that was holding them up immediately decided to cave in. There was a loud groan of metal bending and wood cracking, and the plane slid helplessly down into a dark hole. They fell and crashed hard onto the stone floor below with a loud bang.

At that moment, standing on a balcony at the very far side of the factory complex, Jasper and Casper had just secured the balloon-ship with ropes. They anxiously listened to the loud echo from the crash that boomed through the darkness. A foreboding start.

Dazed, Timmy looked back to make sure Simon was okay. He sat with his paws over his face. Then, as he realized they had finally come to a full stop, he peered out from between his paws and gave another nervous thumbs-up.

They were surrounded by giant iron factory equipment. Shafts of moonlight came down from the broken roof far above.

Timmy suddenly remembered something and

reached into his pocket again. He sighed with relief; the Ziliosphere was still there.

"I think we may have lost the element of surprise," Simon said with a quiet chirp.

"I would have to agree. Terribly sorry about that." Timmy crawled out of the cockpit. "C'mon. Not a moment to lose."

Simon also hopped out, and they rushed down a dark corridor some distance away from the crash site.

"Did you see where the others landed?" Simon whispered.

"Nope. But they can't be too far away."

Timmy and Simon carefully crept forward. They passed several large rooms with high ceilings held up by ornate pillars. Old, abandoned machinery loomed over the boys, like dinosaurs frozen in time. The building smelled of rust and wet stone. They had to tread carefully. In the darkness, Timmy stumbled loudly over pipes jutting out from old equipment. Simon, who was wearing his goggles, fared better.

They were looking for a staircase that led up, since Dobie had mentioned that was probably where the Blue Rabbit kept the children—and Flores, Timmy hoped.

There was also the question of the Rabbit's machine and how they were going to find it and then put a stop to it. Finally, there was the inevitable confrontation with the Blue Rabbit himself . . . a thought that filled Timmy with dread. When the time came to face him, all Timmy could hope to do was his best.

It was then that they heard the familiar noise, but this time it sounded much scarier. Amplified by the stone hallways, the staccato revving of steam-powered

motorcycles echoed loudly through the vast complex. Timmy tried to sense what direction the noise was coming from, but it sounded like he and Simon were being surrounded. Luckily, they had Simon's magical goggles. Simon looked and pointed suddenly to a large door to their left.

"They will come from there," Simon whispered.

Timmy looked around to see if there was a spot that would offer them some kind of advantage, but it was dark and there was no time to think. Instead he withdrew his magic stick and handed it to Simon. Simon nodded in thanks. Timmy then took out the Ziliosphere and held it in his paw. The metal felt cool.

At that moment, the first Iguana rounded the corner. He slid the bike as he came around, kicking up debris through the exhaust steam. He headed straight for them. There was a fixed light on his helmet, like that of a miner's. A second later, seven more Iguana bikers came blasting around the same corner. The high-pitched noise was deafening.

Timmy and Simon stood their ground, both of them in impressive ninja poses. The motorcycles roared. The moonlight gleamed on the iron helmets. Timmy took a breath as he pressed the blue button on the Ziliosphere.

A bright blue light pulsed outward in every direction.

As the light washed over the bikers, it was as if time itself began to crawl. The Iguanas suddenly moved very, very slowly. Their surprised expressions seemed to be happening in slow motion.

It was then a simple thing to walk around and knock them right off their motorbikes one after the other. Timmy and Simon gave them each a gentle shove.

"Do you think they're hurt?" Simon asked.

"They don't look it," said Timmy. "Now let's get a real move on."

They left the Iguanas squirming on the floor in hazy confusion.

Timmy and Simon each grabbed an iron helmet. Simon tightened his chin strap, making sure the helmet sat just right.

Then they each hopped onto one of the motorcycles,

and off they went. Time suddenly returned to normal, and the remaining six bikes, now without riders, regained their normal speed and crashed into the machinery in front of them. The Iguanas, naturally slow animals, could do nothing but sluggishly get up and wave their little arms about.

"Whoa!" Simon exclaimed. "That was amazing!"

"I know! It was like . . . and then they all . . . Just wow!" Timmy was excited beyond words.

"Now let's try to find the others!" Simon yelled.

They sped on, zooming down the hallway until they reached a large winding staircase. Simon shouted over the noise of the engines:

"I think this could be a good look for me. The helmet, I mean. Manly, you know. What do you think? Honestly."

Timmy looked at him in disbelief. "Honestly? Not really," he said back.

"No?"

"No."

"Okay, okay, fine. You have no sense of fashion anyway." Simon looked hurt.

"Okay, I changed my mind. It looks great on you."

"Really?" Simon perked up.

"I mean, I guess so."

"Whatever. Let's go."

Simon revved his engine spitefully and raced up the

stairs. Timmy smiled, shook his head, and followed.

The ride up the steps was more than a bit bumpy. Two stories up, they stopped and listened. They could hear the sounds of running.

"Might be Jasper and Casper," Timmy said.

They continued up in the direction of the sounds. When they reached the next story, they came to a stop and looked around.

In front of them, they saw the balloon-ship moored at a large balcony, but there was no one in the room. The doors stood wide open, and the curtains swayed eerily in the wind, but there was no sign of their friends. The only sound was that of their idling motorcycles. They turned them off and listened. It was quiet. Deadly quiet.

Then:

There was a swooshing sound, and Timmy felt the fur on his nape stand up. Out of the corner of his eye, he saw a figure—no, two figures—come lunging at them from above. With a loud clang to his helmet, Timmy was knocked from his bike, though not nearly as gently

as the Iguanas had been. He was tossed through the air, landed in a failed somersault, and slid across the floor. He saw Simon tumbling the other way. Regaining his footing, although a bit dazed, Timmy sprang up in an intimidating ninja stance.

"Hi*yah*!" He tried to make his voice sound scary.

Two familiar silhouettes rose from the floor twenty feet away.

"Whoops, sorry!" Jasper exclaimed.

"Thought you were the Iguanas!" Casper said.

The piglet brothers looked embarrassed.

"Hope I didn't hurt you," Casper whispered as he came up to Timmy.

"We're okay; no harm done. How about you guys?"

"According to our calculations, we're fine."

Timmy grinned at them.

"Your moves were actually quite nice. Caught us completely by surprise, didn't they, Simon?" Timmy said. "Anyway, it was our fault for coming up on the bikes like that."

Dobie and the cousins now emerged from the shadows.

"Okay, let's regroup," Timmy said. "Has anybody seen the rest of the Iguanas? We just saw eight, but there *must* be more around here somewhere."

"Nope," Casper said. "Not a glimpse of them since we landed."

"Well, they're likely to come at us any moment now, so watch your backs. What about Rabbit? Or the machine?"

Nobody had seen them either.

"We need to find the kids and Flores first," Simon pointed out.

They decided to split up again. There were three more floors above them, and Timmy, Simon, and Jasper would each take a different one. If anyone found the kids, they would return with them to the ship, and the captain would take them down to the city.

Casper and the Gribbles would stay in the room to guard the balloon-ship and fight off the Iguanas, who would almost certainly find them there soon. They would all reunite back at the ship in thirty minutes.

Timmy ran up to the floor just below the top floor and moved quickly among the rooms. He looked for any place that might be appropriate for storing children, although he had no real idea what that kind of room was supposed to look like. He pushed open doors and darted down dark corridors but found only empty rooms.

Finally he came to a long, narrow passageway with iron doors all along one side. He thought it looked very suspicious. He ran along the stone corridor, passing door after door, but none of them had handles or locks. They were just smooth iron doors.

He stopped and banged on one of them, then pressed his ear to the cold, rusty metal. Nothing, not a sound.

There was a brick wall at the far end. At the top, just a little out of his reach, was an iron lever. *It must be for opening the doors,* he thought excitedly. Desperately he looked around for something to stand on, but there was nothing. Sometimes it was a real drag

being short. He walked back a few steps, and then ran at full speed and jumped. On the third try he managed to grab on to the cold metal lever, then just hung there, slowly swinging back and forth. Not weighing very much could be a real drag too. He tried heaving himself up a few times, feeling very silly and hoping that nobody would see him. "This isn't going to work," he muttered.

He changed tactics. Lodging his back paws in the grooves between the bricks, he pulled the lever with all his might. His muscles trembled with the effort. At last, the lever made a metallic moaning sound and came down with a loud snap.

The doors behind him all swung open, groaning against their own weight. Timmy ran to the first door and peered inside.

As soft light from the hallway spilled in, Timmy thought he could see something move on the floor. Then there was more movement farther in. A moment later, a human child sat up and squinted at the light. Then a small elephant boy did the same. Soon, about twenty kids were getting up, as if waking from a deep sleep. They all looked at Timmy curiously. He hadn't made a clear plan for what he was going to do next, but he knew he had to get them all out of there.

"I'm here to help you! Don't be frightened!" he shouted. "We don't have much time!"

Cautiously the kids rose. More of them appeared from the rest of the rooms, and a few minutes later, a hundred kids were crowded around him. A flurry of questions poured out.

"Who are you?"

"Where are we?"

"Why are you dressed like that?"

"Is it lunchtime?"

All Timmy could think of was to try to find Flores among them, but she was nowhere to be seen. He knew

he had to get back to the ship.

"Everyone! Listen to me! Find someone to hold hands with and form a line. And follow me!"

There was some jostling and momentary confusion, but they all managed to do as he had instructed.

He led the long line of kids through the dark rooms

and hallways and down the stairs. The balloon-ship was anchored at the next balcony. It wasn't far.

He suddenly stopped. Below him, between the stairs and the ship, rolling in by the dozens, came the remaining biker Iguanas. They sat on their bikes, revving the engines, blocking the kids' path. There was one at the front. Timmy figured it was Gack. The engine noise

blared rowdily across the big room. Timmy signaled to the kids to stop.

Casper and the Gribble cousins stood at the far end, close to the ship. Just then, Simon and Jasper came down the stairs behind Timmy. They all looked at each other. Then they looked at the Iguanas. There were just so many.

Timmy turned to the kids.

"Walk back up one story and wait there. I promise I'll be back for you all soon. And soon after that, you'll be back with your families," he said. He hoped it would be true.

Timmy pulled out the device, feeling its weight. He remembered that Alfred had told him that it needed time to recharge, so it would be too soon to use it again now. Reluctantly he slid it back into his pocket. It was probably best to save it for the inevitable encounter with the Blue Rabbit anyway.

This was going to have to be done the old-fashioned way. He withdrew his fighting stick.

Exchanging hand signals, they all spread out. Each of them struck a ninja pose and waited.

Within moments, Gack's Iguana bikers revved their engines, spun their wheels, and sped toward the ninjas in a cloud of smoke that smelled like burnt rubber.

The noise was deafening as it bounced all around the big room. Timmy threw himself to the side, avoiding

the first motorcycle while swinging his cane. The Iguana toppled off his bike and crashed to the floor. One down. Through the thick smoke he could see his friends join the fight, like dark shadows moving among the bikes.

It was an epic battle, and although the ninja crime-fighting friends were outnumbered at least five to one, they fought with a passion and ferocity that the Iguanas simply couldn't muster. They dashed quickly through the smoke, attacking like there was no tomorrow. Even Timmy was surprised by how effective they were when working as a team. There were Iguanas being tossed high up into the air, and empty motorcycles that crashed into walls, and iron helmets that rolled across the floor. The ninja gang was unstoppable. *For the kids,* Timmy thought as he attacked, *and for Flores.*

Timmy used all the tricks that his stick could perform, and he even found a few new ones. He learned that he could use it as a pole and swing around and over his opponents. Before the Iguanas had time to react, they had been knocked out by his stick. Jasper and Casper jumped, bounced, and floated in their magic clogs, surprising the Iguanas by suddenly striking from above or landing behind them. They worked in tandem with calculated kicks and chops, finding angles of attack only math-genius pigs could. Simon was fast and lithe, and had apparently practiced several new moves in front of the mirror, which he now used on the Iguanas. He could see through the smoke with his goggles and surprised several of them by springing on them out of nowhere. His paws moved like lightning, delivering fast and accurate punishment. Dobie and the Gribbles, now finally able to use their size to full advantage, proved to be fierce fighters. They would lift an entire motorcycle with an Iguana still on

it and fling it across the room. While spinning and rolling, Timmy saw out of the corner of his eye how Dobie came face to face with Gack. There was a blur of movement.

Then he saw little Gack sail through the air with waving arms as he was tossed into the next hall.

It was one of those fights that, if they had been famous generals and not ninjas (who always fought in secret), bards and musicians would have told stories and composed songs about, and the songs would still have been sung many generations later. As it was, nobody would ever learn of the ninjas heroics that night.

Timmy looked around. All the Iguanas had either fled or lay knocked out across the room. He looked up to where the kids still waited, looking on in awe. He walked up to them and led them downstairs.

They boarded the balloon-ship single file. The captain greeted each of them, and they all sat down on the decks. It was a little crowded, but that was okay. The moorings were loosened, and then the big ship hung there a moment, then turned and floated down into the city.

The friends gathered around again. Simon, who had been on the top floor, said that he had come to a set of tall doors. He had used his goggles to look inside.

"What did you see?" Timmy asked anxiously.

"Nothing. Or rather, the goggles didn't work the way they're supposed to. It was as if they were blocked from seeing inside."

"Hmm . . . very suspicious. It must be the Blue Rabbit's magic."

"Exactly what I thought," Simon said.

"And the Rabbit?"

"No sign of him."

"Okay. Maybe he's already fled." Timmy knew that was probably wishful thinking, and he could feel a shiver go up his spine. "Lead the way, Simon."

They slowly climbed the stairs as quietly as they

could. Soon they reached the top floor and came up
to the doors that Simon had seen. Timmy could feel
his heart beating.

Chapter 16

WITH THE GRIBBLES' help, they pushed the tall doors open, and there stood an enormous gulping and hulking metal contraption. It was even larger than they had imagined. There was a main metal structure of shining brass, with pipes running along its sides. Among the pipes they could see pieces that looked familiar. In the middle were actually pieces they recognized from their orange-peeling machine! The center also had a door, with stairs leading up to it, and lights were blinking on and off within. There was a metal arm attached to one side, which was about to feed glass jars into the body of the machine. *Those must be the jars holding the kids' laughter,* thought Timmy.

On the other side was a mechanism for discarding the empty jars. Smoke puffed from various pipes sticking out of the engine.

Directly in front of the machine stood the Blue

Rabbit. His hands were not moving, his ears were straight up, and his body was absolutely still. He looked at Timmy.

"You took the children. Why did you do that? What was the point? I have already taken their laughter. They are useless to me now. You accomplished nothing."

Timmy, acting much braver than he felt, moved slowly toward him. The Blue Rabbit followed Timmy's every move with his little red eyes.

"The machine is ready," the Rabbit continued. "You don't have the power to stop it. Or me. You defeated my Iguana captains; well done. But you will never be able to defeat me."

"Where is Flores? What did you do to her?"

Rabbit made a grimace that was supposed to look like a smile.

"Ah yes. Your dear cat girlfriend. I considered keeping her alive for a long while. She amused me. But she also upset me. She had a sharp tongue, that one. I can see why you liked her."

Timmy could feel his spirits fall. So that was it. Rabbit had done away with her.

"You killed her!" Timmy yelled.

"Killed her?" Rabbit made that awful laughter-like grimace again. "Why would I do that? I said I considered keeping her alive, and then decided to do so."

Timmy's heart skipped a beat. Rabbit continued:

"But I am afraid she will be coming with me. She is exceptionally smart and good at flying. To me, that is love. Soon I will have a soul, so I will need love. Yes. We will be in love and go away together. It will be perfect."

What a twisted mind this creature had, Timmy thought.

"Where is she?" he snarled.

Rabbit regarded Timmy coolly with his beady little red eyes.

"Why, she's right here."

With that, a trapdoor in the floor slid open, revealing a shallow compartment. Inside, bound, lay Flores. She looked helpless and scared. Instinctively Timmy dashed forward. While doing so, he withdrew the

Ziliosphere. Enough time had passed by then that it should have been fully charged.

He pressed the blue button as he ran, and the blue flash arced over Rabbit. But nothing happened. Time didn't slow, not even a little bit.

Instead the Rabbit snapped his hand up, and it was as if Timmy had run into a wall. He bounced against thin air, was tossed backward, and slid on the slick stone floor.

Simon and the others gasped. They had never seen that kind of magic before. How could they fight against this?

"You are not invited on our trip," Rabbit said calmly.

Then a new voice came from the shadows behind the machine. It was deep, and it echoed over the room.

"Where are you going, Blue Rabbit?" the voice asked.

The Rabbit spun.

"What? Who's there?"

The voice grew in volume.

"Don't you remember me?"
A pause, then:

"Don't you remember your maker?" And now they all recognized the voice. It was Alfred.

Rabbit peered into the shadows, trying to see where Alfred was.

"Yes. Yes, I do."

There was a shift in Rabbit's voice. Something they hadn't heard before. Perhaps a trace of . . . fear?

Timmy had no idea how Alfred had gotten there, but he was sure it had everything to do with magic.

Alfred moved out of the darkness. Because of the lights from the machine, his shadow appeared huge on the wall behind him. He looked larger than they knew him, taller, more imposing. He moved forward, toward Rabbit, and Rabbit took a step back.

"And why are you treating my friends so poorly?" Alfred asked. His voice was big; it echoed and boomed through the room. Rabbit took another step back, then stopped. His hand came up again, like it had with Timmy, but Alfred kept coming toward him.

"Oh no. No, you don't." Alfred's voice now made the windows shake.

Rabbit was quite clearly shocked that his magic wasn't working. They saw that Alfred had his own hand up, countering Rabbit. It was as if a silent but powerful battle of magic was raging between the two of them.

"You may not rob these children of their right to laugh! It's not the way it's done! You sad, miserable

creature!" Alfred's voice boomed. "And you will release the girl."

"I want what all of you already have. I am only doing what I have to!" Rabbit yelled back.

"I'm sorry, Rabbit, but no! Their laughter is not yours to take!"

The walls and floors shook. Everyone stood watching, powerless to intervene. They could all feel the immense energy shifting back and forth, with the two figures fighting for control.

"Now, Timmy!" Alfred said loudly.

Timmy stood, frozen for a second, not sure what Alfred meant.

"Timmy, *now!*"

Timmy finally understood. He rushed forward, toward the machine and toward Flores. This time there was no invisible force field. The Rabbit was too distracted by Alfred. Timmy leapt into the hole where Flores lay. As quickly as he could, he untied her and managed to pull her up onto his back. He jumped up, feeling Flores clinging to him, and dashed across the floor. The others helped her down. Then Timmy turned back to help Alfred.

Alfred was struggling. Rabbit now seemed to have the upper hand.

"Try it now!" Alfred yelled out. "The Ziliosphere!"

Timmy pulled out the device and pressed the

button. Nothing happened, not even a spark. Timmy could feel his heart sink. He watched as Alfred fell to the ground and the Blue Rabbit strode forward.

Suddenly there was a bright flash, nearly blinding Timmy, and a sparkling plume of a million colors shot out of the blue device like fireworks. The plume engulfed Rabbit. Sparks and smoke filled the room.

Timmy could see the Rabbit's movements start to slow, but not very much. The Blue Rabbit's power was great.

"His neck! There is a switch under the fur!" Alfred called out again through the sparkles that were still raining down. Timmy could see that he was barely hanging on.

Timmy ran forward again, straight at Rabbit. Simon, Jasper, and Casper were right behind him. Together they made a ladder with their bodies, with Timmy on the top.

He reached into the blue fur on Rabbit's neck. He felt a flap and pushed it up. Inside was a switch.

"Flip it! Quickly! I can't hold on!" Alfred was shaking now.

It was an old iron switch, and at first it wouldn't budge. The Rabbit started turning. The friends scrambled below Timmy to follow Rabbit's rotation, and Timmy almost fell. He pressed the switch with all the might he had in his little paw, and at last he could feel it loosen from its rusted casing.

Flop! And at once everything changed. The Rabbit gave a jolt and let out a horrible howl that ricocheted around the room. Very slowly Rabbit started to sink to the floor.

In a beat, Alfred had rushed up to him and was now holding Rabbit up, very tenderly, so that he wouldn't fall. Alfred held the furry toy in his arms and gazed into his eyes. Timmy could see that Alfred looked very sad.

"This is not the way it's done, my old friend," Alfred said softly to his creation.

Then he very carefully laid Rabbit down on the floor. Alfred exhaled deeply. The Blue Rabbit lay perfectly still; his eyes were closed. Timmy watched Alfred. His eyes were sad, and his lips moved, as if he was whispering. Timmy realized he was saying goodbye. Timmy waited a moment, and then he walked up to the old toymaker.

"Are you okay, Alfred?"

"Yes, Timmy, I'm fine, just fine. Well done, all of you." His voice was still serious.

"We got him," Timmy said.

"You got him. You all got him." Alfred's face finally broke into a soft smile, and he looked at the young friends. They were a gang of ninja crime-fighting animal inventors, and together they had saved the city.

Timmy saw Flores, who had now gotten to her feet.

He walked up to her and took her paws in his. She looked tired, but she was smiling at him.

"You silly cat," she said, but her eyes said something else.

"I'm not the one who got herself captured."

"Just so that you would come for me, oh ninja master. I couldn't make it too easy for you." She smiled mischievously.

They looked into each other's eyes and stood nose to nose. Behind them, they noticed everyone watching in anticipation. It was a little awkward, but neither of them cared.

And then Timmy and Flores kissed. The room broke out in a cheer. It was quite the moment. They finally let each other go and turned back to their friends.

"So what now?" Timmy asked.

"Well, now help me open all those jars so all those poor kids can get their given right to laugh back." Alfred smiled.

Alfred unhooked jar after jar from the machine and handed them down to the friends. There were hundreds of them, and everyone helped unscrew the lids.

As each jar was opened, a faint laugh could be heard somewhere across the city. There were probably many startled parents that night who woke from their sleep and suddenly heard their kids burst into uncontrollable laughter.

With his head down and feeling a little ashamed, Timmy had to tell Flores that he had crashed her airplane. At first her eyes narrowed and she looked at him very sternly; then she burst out in a laugh and said:

"Well, then you'll just have to help me build a new one! With lots of magical gear in it this time."

Later, the captain came back with the balloon-ship, and they all got on board. Alfred boarded last, carrying the Blue Rabbit gently in his arms. As the sun started to peek over the mountaintops early that morning, they sailed the giant airship down through the clouds, high over the streets and squares of Elyzandrium, and back home.

Timmy and Flores found an attic across the street from the toymaker's shop, where they moved in together. Dobie and the Gribble cousins already lived just a few blocks over, so they stayed where they were. Alfred put the Blue Rabbit into a large box, which he put into a room in the very rear of his shop. He locked the room with several heavy locks. You couldn't be too safe. Simon, Jasper, and Casper moved their stuff from the baker's loft and found a space just a few buildings away from the old toy shop. While they carried their equipment down the stairs, the baker's daughter, Mathilda, stood watching them. Simon told one of his jokes, and Mathilda burst out in a wonderful little laugh.

All the friends spent their days in the back rooms of Alfred's shop and helped him build amazing magical toys. But when night fell, they would still patrol the rooftops of the city, watching for any bad guys and keeping the city safe. The Gribbles finally became full members of the gang, after having lifted many heavy things in Alfred's workshop and having come with countless boxes of chocolate. They also all finally voted on what the name of their gang should be, and they became the Magical Ninjas. Timmy thought the name was quite nice.

It was during a particularly stormy night about a month later when something very strange happened. Despite the weather, the gang was out patrolling as usual. Through the rain, they suddenly saw something. At first it was a mere speck in the sky, barely visible through the downpour, but as lightning flashed, they saw what it was: a bird—round and fat, and with wings that looked much too small to carry it—fluttering through the air. An object of some kind was strapped to its back. The bird struggled against the strong winds, seemingly utterly exhausted. As they watched, the fat bird fell slowly from the night sky.

"Come on!" Timmy shouted.

They all ran toward where the bird had fallen. When they reached it, they could see it lying there, barely conscious, breathing heavily. It looked at them with defeat in its eyes. Simon approached it carefully, knelt down, and petted it gently. He gave it some water, and it seemed to smile at him, and a minute later it had fallen asleep in his arms. The friends then focused their attention on the object on the bird's back, which turned out to be a container of some sort. Timmy opened it carefully. Within was a rolled-up piece of paper, which he unfolded. It was a message, written in a language he had never seen before, but among the words he didn't understand, there was a name he knew:

Alfred.

The friends looked at each other. This had to be a message for him! But what could it mean?

Acknowledgments

This book owes its existence to imagination itself, which has prodded me and dared me to chase it all of my life. I also must thank my family—my wonderful parents, Robert and Ing-Marie; my amazing brother, Martin, and his wife, Anna, and children, Vilma and Hjalmar; and my brilliant aunt Carina—who have watched with often amused bewilderment my twisty, bumpy, and odd path through life. I have always had their unwavering support, even if it has taken years to explain to them what it is I actually do. And of course to my extraordinary Dannah, who patiently believed and loved. Many thanks to all the excellent people at Delacorte Press/Random House, who took a chance on this work, and much gratitude to my friend Monica Stein at Bonnier Carlsen, who championed the book in its first rendition.

About the Author

HENRIK TAMM is a conceptual designer in Hollywood involved in various animated and live-action projects. He has helped create the worlds of such popular and acclaimed films as *Shrek* and the Chronicles of Narnia series. Although written originally in English, this novel was initially published in Swedish in his home country of Sweden. *Ninja Timmy* is Henrik Tamm's first adventure in book form.

Visit Ninja Timmy on Facebook